This book belongs to:

_____

Almondine grows up

Gabriele Zucchelli

Acknowledgements:

Huge thanks to Ian Long and Deborah Murrell
for their invaluable contribution.

BOOKS

Published by GZ Books

Print Book ISBN: 978-1-8383209-2-8

ePub ISBN: 978-1-8383209-3-5

www.almondine.club

Special thanks:

Julia & Montserrat

Contents

Prologue

What's it like to be a teenager?

I bet you are looking forward to being a bit older and starting to have more freedom!

And so was our tiny Almondine. She has her own story to tell, one that changed her forever. Because she didn't just change; she completely transformed.

Chapter 1

I'm Almondine

I'm Almondine.

Alma gave me this name because she found me inside an almond. That's where I came from.

Life with Alma was great. We had lots of fun.

And then everything changed. It only took one little mistake.

All because I didn't listen to the one person who really loves me.

Alma is a girl like me, but huge. Everyone else is huge too, so I suppose I'm the weird one. But being small has never bothered me. It's actually been a joy to explore Alma's gigantic world, although sometimes I made her cross and she often told me that I was too naughty for my size. Alma is my friend and my mum. She's also the only person who knows that I exist. She always worried I'd be in serious danger if I were to be discovered. So, aside from Alma, there was nobody else for me to play with, or to share my adventures.

For a while, Alma and I had a lot of fun together, even if we did get into trouble sometimes.

But then one day, everything changed. I remember staring at the garden from her window and thinking how much I'd like to live out there, in the open. I wanted to be in the wild, maybe because I felt a bit wild myself. You see, I loved Alma but she made me feel almost like one of her toys. She didn't get it.

I told her I'd grown up so, why couldn't she respect that?

I really wanted to move into her garden playhouse and live there on my own. Instead, I ended up being locked up again in her bedside table drawer. It made me so upset that I stopped talking to her.

In the end, Alma gave me my freedom and even helped me to prepare my new home. In return, I promised to behave and always listen to her advice. It felt good that she trusted me.

I got so excited, I even forgot about the withered flower on my head and the weird leaves sprouting through my hair.

You see, I haven't told you yet, but I was going

13

through some kind of transformation.

Now I know very well what was happening to me, but at the time I had no idea. Back then I really couldn't care less, because finally I had what I wanted: my freedom!

But I hadn't learned yet how to use this freedom.

Chapter 2

My New Friends

For the first time in my life, I had my own place, deep inside our beautiful garden. I can still remember how happy it made me to live there! But it was when I felt happiest that I suddenly lost everything.

I slept on a wooden shelf in the playhouse. It was very cosy: my bed was an old cooking spoon, complete with a pillow and a blanket. Alma cut out a box to be my private bedroom, gave me my own wardrobe, and I even had a sort of kitchen to make food.

This was mostly for fun. I don't really cook, you

16

see. I just eat earth: plain, moist, preferably clayish earth. It can taste so delicious sprinkled with old wood, mixed with peat moss or stuffed with worm poo cupcakes!

I know you big humans think I'm weird, and that for you earth would be the most disgusting thing to put in your mouth. I suppose it wouldn't be good for your stomach. But that's what I eat, and Alma didn't mind at all: I grew up being spoon-fed soil from a flowerpot. She knew exactly what I liked, and she became so good at picking out the best bits.

Alma helped me store my favourite earth in small jars, and I served myself from them three times a day. And I wasn't the only one who liked it.

I started sharing it with some of my little friends, who seemed to enjoy my meals as much as I did: a family of roly-polies and their weird millipede uncle. They were always very hungry and never said thank you. They were simple creatures in that way. When I decided that they'd gorged themselves enough on my food, I used to poke them off the shelf. They'd coil into balls and land painlessly on the floor, bouncing a few times. Then they'd uncoil and crawl away between the floorboards, only to come back again the next day

with more of their relatives.
That way, I made lots of friends.
There was Big Mama Spider, who
terrified Alma each time
she saw her. But she
didn't mean any
harm – she'd even
scratch my back
before bed. There was
Daddy Long Legs
who'd never leave
the ceiling.
And then there
were the moths!

Herald, Gypsy, chatty Emmelina with her funny,
pointy wings, and Tabby, who was always teasing
Etiella for the horn on her head. Some, like Tabby
and Gypsy, were very hairy, and I loved stroking
their furry backs as if they were my pets.

And then there was Stinky, the green shield-bug,
who wasn't all that popular, Gonzo, the lazy
bumblebee, who'd sometimes stay for the night,
and Zippy, the hoverfly.

Some slept during the day, some slept at night.
They all came in through a small knothole at the
end of the wall, a little round passage that was our

only gateway into the garden, since the main door was always shut. I often stared at this hole, thinking about going out through it one day, too. It seemed such a normal thing for all the others to do, so what could go wrong? I knew Alma would be disappointed if I didn't keep my word to stay inside the playhouse at all times.

But, after a while, my longing to leave grew too hard to resist.

Chapter 3

Brave New World

Every day, Alma told me how careful I had to be now that I was living on my own, and warned me about potential disasters. She said I was small and defenceless, so I must never, ever leave the playhouse.

In fact, she said the same things so many times that I began to ignore her. She just wanted to keep me for herself, I thought – always putting me down, never giving me a word of encouragement.

Now I know that she just wanted the best for me, and it was a mistake to think otherwise.

I used to stare out of the playhouse window and

watch all the things that were happening in the garden. It seemed so still, and yet so full of life: blue tits and sparrows flashing from branch to branch, squirrels digging, bees and butterflies savouring flowers, and ladybirds, flies and other tiny insects everywhere. At night there were bats, flitting quickly through the air. I even spotted a couple of fireflies! These creatures all looked amazing to me. All unique, and free to go wherever they wanted.

What's the point of living outside if I'm stuck in a house again? I thought.

If I was going to get out, it seemed that it would be safer to do it at night, when my moth friends could keep an eye on me.

So one night I gathered up all my courage, squeezed through the knothole and got into the garden, my heart pounding with fear and excitement.

I walked through the grass with the moths flying all around me.

I reached the spot where I remembered seeing the fireflies, and there they were. And there were also so many other little creatures that I hadn't been able to see from the house.

I was amazed: all this life around me, the trees gently rocking in the breeze, the stars high above. I felt truly free. I wandered through the grass, over the paving stones and into the strawberry patch.

Before long my hesitant steps turned into a strut and then into a skip, until I was running and jumping around all over the place, chasing bugs, climbing on flowers and snacking on the most delicious bits of soil I could find.

After that, I escaped every night. My secret excursions became longer each time, until I only got back just before sunrise, tired and dirty. I made friends with every creature in my garden.

Even the squirrels would come down from the trees, greet me with a bow, and offer me a hazelnut. I had no idea why they did that.

After a while Alma started to notice I was leaving my home untidy. To be honest, I'd lost interest in it. At first, Alma joked about my messy behaviour and helped me to tidy the place up. But she soon started to wonder what I was up to. She said I hadn't been the same since I left her room. I told her I was happy, that I was having the time of my life, and I asked her why she wasn't happy for me. We had another argument and when I told her to leave me alone she broke down in tears.

After she left I saw Spritz from my window: one of

our neighbour's cats, who sometimes visited our garden. He was standing at the edge of the lawn, and we stared at each other for a long time.

He looked so mysterious, with his deep, soft fur, his long whiskers, his short cuddly ears and those bright blue eyes.

I wished I could ride on the back of his neck, holding onto his red collar and letting him take me away to discover all the gardens outside our fence, and far beyond.

Unfortunately, he was thinking of doing the exact same thing.

Chapter 4

Spritz

It must have been around midday when I was woken up by a scratching sound.

I was expecting to see Alma, coming to make up for yesterday's argument.

I rubbed my heavy eyes and saw Spritz balancing on the little balustrade of the playhouse window, peering inside, and gently stroking the glass with his paw.

He looked so cute and cuddly, I got up and ran over to him.

'Spritz?'

Even though I was a bit scared, I couldn't help

smiling when he looked at me.

I touched the window and so did he, meowing. His big blue eyes were so close to mine. Did he want to play? It seemed like he was pleading with me to come outside.

My mind was racing: what was I supposed to do?

I knew what Alma would have said. Instead, I grabbed one of the hazelnuts the squirrel gave me and ran to the knothole.

I walked around the house and I saw him, still peering inside the window.

'Spritz?'

He immediately leapt on to the ground. The
closer he got the slower he moved, his head
stretched forward with curiosity, his blue eyes
focused on me. When I showed him the hazelnut
he backed off for a moment. Then he sat down.
'Do you want to play with me?' I said.
I threw the nut in front of him. He watched it
drop, then looked back at me.
'Don't you like playing with marbles?' I asked,
inching toward him.
He raised his paw, as if to say that I was too close
to him. I stroked it. It was very soft, just as I had
imagined. And he was so big! He gently tapped me
twice on the shoulder. Then came a much heavier

blow, which knocked me to the ground.

I chuckled. I remember thinking that I had to teach him how to be gentle with me. I got up.

'You big, clumsy clown!' I said. 'Careful with those fat feet of yours! I'm not the ball.'

I went to pick up the hazelnut, saying, 'Let's try again.'

But Spritz swiped at me, throwing me on to the ground again.

I was angry this time and I marched towards him, determined to pull his whiskers. Spritz saw me coming and backed away, as if I had scared him.

I started to tell him off and he stood up to listen. I wasn't sure if he understood me, though, as he didn't say anything. I was still attracted to his beautiful, soft fur, and I couldn't wait for the chance to persuade him to let me climb on his neck.

Spritz sat down again, and looked away.

'What are you looking at?' I said. 'I'm here! I'm talking to you.'

He still wasn't paying attention.

'Did I offend you? Listen, it's fine… just be careful, OK? We can play with something else if you want.'

I picked up the nut and showed it to him again.

But this time he pounced, and pinned me to the ground with both paws. Then he grabbed me in his mouth and ran off.

Chapter 5

Prisoner

Spritz quickly climbed our fence and carried me across the other gardens, where my imagination had often taken me. But I wasn't riding on his back – I was clenched between his pointy fangs. 'Put me down!' I shouted. He ignored me and carried on, scaling fence after fence with surprising agility. I was dizzy from being shaken in his mouth and my eyesight began to blur. I was still telling him to stop when I lost my breath and passed out.

When I regained consciousness I found myself inside an empty bucket. I got up and felt my chest

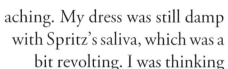

aching. My dress was still damp with Spritz's saliva, which was a bit revolting. I was thinking about taking the dress off when, suddenly, a little furry creature quickly circled twice around the bucket, jumping over the twigs and empty snail shells that lay beside it. Before I could see what it was, it had already disappeared under a pile of dead leaves and seemed to be trembling in its hiding place.

'Hello? Who are you?' I said. 'Come out. Did Spritz bring you here, too?'

I stepped towards the creature.

It darted out again, then zig-zagged around me, sniffed me and finally stood on its hind legs, quivering its whiskers. It was a young boy-mouse.

'Squee! What are you?' he asked, in a thin, squeaky little voice.

'I'm Almondine,' I said. 'And you? Tell me, what's your name?'

'What's an Almond-squee?' he said, considering

my reply. 'You look a bit like a human.'

'Almondine is my name. I suppose I am sort of a human, but I'm not really…'

'You have leaves on your head-squee,' he said.

'Oh, those are actually part of me,' I explained.

'Part of you-squee? How?'

'They just grow out of me. Like your fur grows out of you.'

'Tos-squee, what is this?' he asked, rushing back to the little mound of leaves and talking to someone who seemed to be hiding there. 'Tos-squee, Tos-squee! There's something to see-squee!'

The mouse pulled some leaves aside with its paws and uncovered a friendly-looking brown toad.

'Tos-squee, do we need to kill the Almond-squee?'

'Hey, excuse me!' I said. 'What do you mean by that, exactly?!'

'Naaaaaa,' the toad rasped.

'But she is a human, Tos-squee! A little human with leaves-squee.'

'She means no haaaaarm. She is good.'

The mouse came closer, and after looking me over for a second time, he gave me a push.

'What did you do that for?' I asked.

It seemed as though he was provoking me and waiting to see how I'd react. I couldn't believe the

cheek of the little fellow.
'So... do you think we-squee can trust the Almond-squee?' he asked the toad again.

'Hurp.'

'All right, then I won't kill you,' he said. A smile twitched his whiskers.

Then the mouse leapt on to me, pulled at my leaves and laughed.

'You're very funny-squee,' he said.

I found myself holding him in my arms like a baby, and he hugged me. It was a surprise how he'd suddenly warmed to me.

'What's your name?' I asked, as I lowered him on to the floor.

'Orzo. And she is Tos-squee. She can't move very well. She has a broken leg-squee.'

'Hello, Tos-squee,' I said.

'It's Toscaaaa!'

'I mean Tosca. Is your leg really broken? Can I have a look?'

I looked, and one of her hind legs did look twisted.

34

'Poor you,' I said gently reaching for her wounded leg to examine it. 'We need to tie a stick around it.' But as soon as I touched her skin, she squirted something on to my feet and dress.

'Sorry. It aaaaalways happens when I'm touched.'

'It's OK,' I said, shaking my feet to let the liquid drip off. It had a strong smell, and it stung my skin a bit.

'I'm not sure if I can help,' I said. 'Does it hurt you very much?'

'Nothing hurts me.'

'Really? That's hard to believe.'

'Not aaaaany more.'

'Well… I'll try to fix you up,' I reassured her.

I noticed that Orzo was now stalking a fly. He leapt up and caught it in his mouth, only to spit it straight out again.

'What's he doing?'

'Traaaaaining.'

I was puzzled. 'What do you mean?'

'To beat the caaaaat when it'll come baaaaack again,' Tosca replied.

'You are joking, aren't you? He's tiny. Spritz will bash him to bits!'

'I know. Isn't it saaaaad?' Tosca said, expressionlessly. 'We'll aaaaaall be killed, aaaaanyway, so it doesn't really maaaatter,' she went on.

Chapter 6

A Splash of Pee

I was stuck in a bucket, about to be torn apart by Spritz, and in the company of two crackpots. But I wasn't just going to wait for Spritz to kill us all. I had to think of an idea, and fast.

I looked at Orzo and Tosca, and the empty snail shells lying around. And that's when I thought of something.

I picked up an empty shell, placed it behind Tosca's body, and started rubbing her thigh.

She flinched, and some of her horrible liquid squirted into the shell. Soon, it was full.

'Here, Orzo. This is for you,' I said, handing it to

him. 'It'll be your weapon against Spritz.'

'What? A snail shell full of Tos-squee's pee-squee?
I want to fight him with my own claws-squee!'

'That's all very well, Orzo, but you're too small.
Believe me, there's no other way,' I said filling
another shell for myself. 'When Spritz comes
back, this is what we'll do.'

I explained my plan to them, then we sat next to
each other, waiting.

There was a beautiful sky overhead. Birds darted
from tree to tree, and bees hovered over flowers.
Orzo yawned and fell asleep.

'How did Spritz find you?' I asked Tosca.

'On the roaaad. Aaaaaafter a storm. I got lost.

Shouldn't have left the paaaaark.'

'I should have stayed in my home, too. I wish I'd listened to Alma.'

'Aaaaalma?' Tosca repeated.

'She's my mum. Sort of. What about you, do you have a mum?'

'I aaaaam a mum. Or I waaaaaas.'

'Oh… your children must miss you. Where are they now?'

'I don't know.'

'Why not?'

'We toads don't look aaaaaafter our taaadpoles. We just laaaaay eggs and they go. Thaaaaat's that.'

'That's kind of sad… to be abandoned by your children, I mean. It's not very nice.'

'So it waaaaas with my mum. I did just the saaaaame.'

'But how could you?

'Taaaaadpoles have little braaaaains.'

'Do you still miss them?'

'Aaaaaah – yes, I do. But they may be dead, for aaall I know. Hurp,' she sighed.

'Oh dear, Tosca! Don't say that! I'll help you find them again.'

Tosca looked at me as if I was mad, and didn't speak another word.

The sky began to darken.
We were both dozing off when
Spritz's face suddenly appeared
over the rim of the bucket.
We woke up with a start. Orzo
accidentally dropped his shell,
spilling the pee; then he ran along
the edge of the bucket in a circle.
Spritz followed him with his eyes,
then reached down to catch him.
'Over here! Look at me!' I shouted.
I waved one arm, holding my shell
with the other.
'Oi, you! Useless ball of hair! Look over here!'
Orzo hid behind Tosca, who remained unfazed by
the commotion.
Spritz shifted his attention to me.
'Yes… look at my wiggly arm! Come and play
with me!' I shouted.
He didn't wait. He leaned over and seized me in
his mouth.
As he pulled me out of the bucket, I grabbed the
shell with both hands and splashed Tosca's nasty
pee into his eyes.
Spritz made a loud 'Meee-uugghhh!' kind of
sound. He sprang up in the air like a grasshopper

and tipped the bucket over with its paws, dropping me on the ground.

He shook his head a few times, so hard that it looked as if his ears might fly off. Then he shot madly over the fence into the next garden and disappeared.

The bucket had landed upside down. I knocked on it with my fist.

'You OK in there?'

'Me-squee? Yes!' Orzo shouted.

I searched around me and found a dry stick. Using it as a lever, I managed to lift the bucket just enough for Orzo to squeeze out.

'Come on, Tosca, you too! Get out!' I called. 'Orzo, help me push the edge of the bucket a bit higher up! Tosca, out now!'

'Hurp. Whaaaaatever,' she croaked.

'Don't hurp me! We aren't leaving without you!' I said.

Tosca slowly dragged herself outside the bucket and we finally let it drop back.

'Now whaaaaat?' Tosca asked.

Chapter 7

Saved by a Ball

We were at the end of a big, overgrown garden.
'I know where to go! Follow me-squee!' said Orzo,
decisively.
'Do you? Thank goodness for that,' I said. 'Let's
get away from here.'
It was obvious that Tosca wasn't going to be able
to walk very far. So I hauled her onto my back. She
was heavy, but I could just about carry her.
I followed Orzo, but I could barely keep up with
his rapid changes of direction. He seemed on top
of the world: scurrying, sniffing, and climbing up
shrubs to see the way.

When we'd squeezed under three fences and crossed three gardens, Orzo finally stopped for a moment under a shrub below a brick wall.

'Hee-hee-hee-squee! That was fun!'

'Where are we now, Orzo?' I asked, panting.

'Don't ask me-squee!'

'But I was following you! I thought you knew where you were going!'

'So did I-squee. But what does it matter? Let's carry on!'

'No, wait. Excuse me, what do you mean by what does it matter?!'

'He's right. Hurp. It doesn't maaaaatter,' Tosca commented with a croak.

'Tosca, you don't get to comment, since I'm carrying you. Orzo, did you really know where we were going all that time?' I insisted.

'No. But we went a long way, didn't we-squee?

Let's keep moving!'

'I'm not following you if you don't know where you're going,' I said, letting Tosca down.

There was a lawn in front of the wall where we were standing, surrounded by small trees. We could have been anywhere.

Then Orzo pointed to the end of the garden.

Spritz was walking in our direction along the top of the fence, still shaking his head.

Orzo hid behind Tosca.

'He-squee… he-squee… he's been following us-squee,' he stammered.

'We'll aaall die, I haaaaave told you. Hurp,' said Tosca flatly.

'No, we won't,' I whispered, gesturing at them to hush. 'If we run, he'll see us moving. The grass is too short. He'll catch up with us fast. We've got to find somewhere to hide.'

'Hide where-squee?'

'Here, come with me. Slowly,' I replied.

There was a sunflower stalk close to us. I reached up for a leaf and slowly pulled it down.

'Both of you, stand behind me,' I said, sneaking a look at Spritz.

The cat had hopped off the fence. He was licking his paws and cleaning his face again.

'Tos-squee – you wet me-squee,' Orzo hissed.

'Hurp. Well, you touched me,' Tosca said.

'Shut up, both of you,' I whispered.

Spritz looked in our direction and began pacing toward us.

'He's heard us,' I said.

He was only a few steps away from us when two boys came running into the garden with a football.

They kicked the ball against the brick wall. It missed us by a hair and bounced back near them. Spritz cowered in the grass.

'Hey, look! The cat!' one of the boys shouted.

He took aim at Spritz, but before he could hit the ball, the cat scooted off down the garden. The boys laughed.

'You're so mean!' one of them said.

'Did you see how fast he ran?' the other replied.

The boys kept kicking the ball against the wall,

and we jumped with each thundering impact around us.

'It's too dangerous here!' I said.

Orzo didn't wait to be told again, and scurried off in the opposite direction to the one Spritz had fled in. I picked up Tosca and rushed off too.

'Hey, what's that?' one of the boys said.

'What?'

'I just saw a toad walking on two legs.'

'You must be hallucinating,' said the other one.

'Look, there it is! It just went under there!' the first boy shouted.

We all hid under a heather shrub.

'I'm telling you, it's in here,' said the boy, pulling

some branches aside.

The other boy joined in with the search, but without much interest. After a while, he gave up. 'Let's go back to play,' he said as he started to juggle the ball. And the search stopped there.

As soon as they turned their backs, I picked up Tosca again and we ran across the garden to the next fence. We squeezed through a small gap and entered yet another garden.

I stopped and put Tosca down for a moment.

'Wow... That was so close-squee,' Orzo said, all excited. 'What fun-squee!'

'It didn't seem like you were having... so much fun at the time...' I said, still panting.

It was already getting dark and we had to keep

49

50

moving. I hoisted Tosca on my back once again and we continued our trek into the unknown.

Not long afterwards, we reached a long slope covered in brambles and litter.

'What's this place-squee?' Orzo asked.

'No idea, but these thorns should keep us safe from Spritz,' I said.

Suddenly, there was a loud roar and a tooting sound. I looked down the slope and saw what looked like a huge metal snake slithering out of a tunnel. We were standing above the steep embankment of a railway line.

Chapter 8

Shelter in the Rubbish

It was late, and we needed a shelter for the night. Amongst the litter, I found a plastic milk bottle with a hole big enough for us to get in.

'We'll sleep in here,' I decided. 'It'll keep us safe. I hope.'

'Just a minute,' said Orzo.

He ran into the bramble bushes, then emerged with four blackberries.

'For our dinner-squee,' he said as he slipped inside the bottle.

We'd gone through enough for one day. I was exhausted, and couldn't wait to rest.

I went to help Tosca get inside and saw how painfully she was dragging her injured leg behind her. I needed to do something about it, so I snapped a stalk to the right length  and tied it around her limb with blades of grass. Then I pushed her into our hideout. I took one last look around. It was a nice, warm evening: insects were in the air, and bats were flitting in and out of the tunnel. All around me, the lush greenery clashed with the jarring colours of the plastic rubbish scattered everywhere. Humans had thrown this stuff from the road nearby. It was awful, and it made me sad. Why would they do that? And yet I was relieved that a piece of this ugly waste was going to give us a safe haven for the night. Or so I thought.

I squeezed in. It felt really small inside. It was so dark that I could barely see my companions, and I tripped over Tosca's leg.

'Hurp!' she moaned, lazily.

'Sorry!' I tried to go another way, but squeezed Orzo instead.

'Careful with my berries! You just squee-shed one!' he complained.

'Sorry, Orzo – move down, please,' I said. 'And Tosca, please don't pee in here.'

'Not up to me,' she replied.

'Well… Just stay calm,' I replied.

The bottle rocked as we each made our adjustments, until we'd finally made ourselves comfortable enough in our own spots to try to get to sleep.

'I know where we-squee can go tomorrow!' said the young mouse, chewing on a berry.

'Orzo, go to sleep,' I said. I could feel my eyes getting heavy.

'We need a dog-squee!' Orzo said. 'Not too big… a nice one. I'll tell him all about that nasty cat, so he can hold it back while I grab its face-squee with my claws-squee, and…'

'Orzo, sleep…' I slurred.

'I'll tear his face-squee! I'll pull out his eyes-squee!

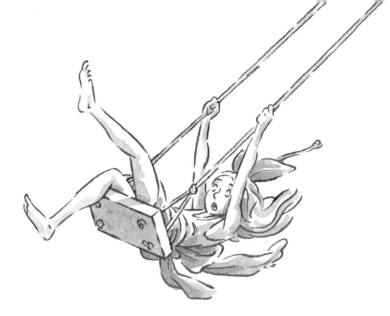

And then-squee, when he's begging for mercy, I'll come back to rescue you. We'll stay together, we'll find our way home-squee… and then we'll look for…' his words dwindled away as I fell asleep.

I dreamt that Alma took me to our old room, put me inside the doll's house and rocked me on a swing. It was lovely and reassuring. Then she started pushing me too fast. I asked her to stop, but she wouldn't listen. She started laughing in a nasty, angry way that shook the whole doll's house. Everything was falling on me. Why was she doing this? I kept asking her to stop, but she went on banging the doll's house and pushing me around, until I woke up with a start.

Our bottle was moving violently in all directions.

Awful snarls started coming from outside.

'What's going on?' Orzo shouted as he fell over me. 'Help me-squee!'

'Someone outside wants to get us!' I shouted.

Another abrupt jolt made me and Orzo roll on top of Tosca.

'Hurp. This is when we die,' the toad said placidly, before squirting the back of the bottle.

'Ah! Squee-yuck!' Orzo shouted.

The situation was getting unbearable. A big black nose tried to squeeze in through the hole. It felt like the bottle was being pushed over stones, making us all bounce around.

The nose started sniffing loudly. Then, suddenly, it pulled away.

A series of huge sneezes came from outside. We heard footfalls padding away. Peace returned.

It seemed that Tosca's smell had put the animal off. She'd saved our lives again.

I peered out of the bottle. In the distance, under the feeble glow of the moon, the silhouette of a fox was disappearing into the night.

'I don't think it'll be back any time soon,' I said. Orzo pushed himself out.

'I'm soaked!!' he cried. 'Squee-yuck! I'm not going back in there!'

I looked inside the bottle to see if Tosca was OK.
She just croaked, 'Hurp...'
'You see, we didn't die,' I said.

'Whaaaaatever.'
'Not whatever! I want this stuff off me-squee!'
Orzo complained.
'Just roll on the ground, Orzo. It'll get rid of the
smell and sting.'
I showed him how to do it, and soon we were both
properly filthy. It made me a bit peckish, so I
gobbled a handful or two of soil.

'Squee-eeek! Did you really squee-eat that?' Orzo shouted, shocked.

'Yes!' I said, forgetting that it seemed weird to some people. 'You should try it.'

This made him laugh.

We leaned against the bottle and slowly calmed down. Under the moonlight, surrounded by the buzzing drone of crickets, we tried to rest again.

Until around dawn, when a sharp twittering sound woke us up again.

Chapter 9

Red-Red

A robin was standing right in front of us.

'Hi, nice to meet you,' I said.

'Trrr-trrr… teee-teee-teee-tweeeee… You-two… you-two… are standing on my breakfast!' the bird said, annoyed.

'What do you mean? What meal?'

I got up and looked around: there was nothing under either my or Orzo's feet. The bottle was resting on a patch of earth surrounded by a cardboard box and other litter.

'Teee-tweee-trrr… I come here… to eat… every morning. Trrr-tweee! And you're on it!'

He hopped closer to us and fluffed his feathers to make himself look bigger. I backed away. Although the bird was little, he was fearless. He pecked the bottle, then looked at me. I grabbed the handle near the hole and pulled the heavy container slightly to one side: it revealed a patch of soil covered in cornflakes from a nearby box.

The robin hopped on to it and dug out an earthworm, which he swallowed in one quick greedy gulp.

'Nice… trrr… tweee-teee.'

I moved the bottle even further away.

'I'm sorry,' I said. 'There you go, see if there are any more.'

'Teee-tweee… Thank you,' he said.

He was scanning the earth when Tosca slowly

climbed out of the bottle and joined us. We all watched the little bird busy having his breakfast. 'Robin? Erm... Excuse me,' I said. 'We're actually lost. Is there any chance you could help us find our way home?'

The robin turned towards us with another earthworm wriggling in his beak. He quickly swallowed it and hopped in front of Tosca.

'Trrr-teee-teee-tweeee... Your kind doesn't have a home... trrr... sorry,' he said.

Tosca didn't even reply.

I was sure she must have had a home, but before I could say anything, the robin hopped right in front of me.

'Tweeeee-teee-teee-trrr... As to you... I don't

know what you are! I can't help you. Trrr,' he
declared.

Then he hopped in front of Orzo.

'Trrr-tweee-teee-teee… Your home? Your home
is underneath a house, isn't it, trrr?' he asked.

'Yes-squee! How did you know?' Orzo said.

'Tweee… What colour is the door?'

'Red! It has a red door!'

The robin fluttered with excitement.

'Trrrr! Red! But what red? Worm-Red?
Hollyberry-Red? Blackberry-Red? Trrr?' Or just
Robin-Red?'

'Squee-erm… maybe Robin-Red?' Orzo replied,
hesitantly.

'Robin-Red? Teee-teee-trrr… Black grille under
Robin-Red door?'

'Yes-squee! To get in, we go through a black grille
under the door!'

'Then… I know! Trrr-tweeeee…
Follow meee!'

The robin was about
to take off when he
turned back and
saw Tosca.

'What's she doing?
Trrrr…'

63

Tosca was standing among the cornflakes, chewing. When she saw the robin looking at her, she stopped.

'Trrr-tweeee… Is she stealing my breakfast?'

'Of course not, she's just curious. Let's go!' I replied, lifting Tosca on to my back.

'Tweee-teee-teeeee… I don't like toads… Trrr.' The robin started flying from one branch to another.

'Wait! Not so quick!' I shouted as I ran below, trying to follow him.

'What made you steal his worms?' I whispered to Tosca. 'He might not have helped us if he'd known what you were doing!'

'I waaaas hungry,' she said.

'Lucky he didn't see you…' I said, following Orzo and the robin. 'How's your leg now?'

'Whaaatever,' she croaked, listlessly.

'Really, Tosca. You're absolutely hopeless!'

We squeezed through some bramble bushes and hopped over cans and litter until we'd left the hill near the railway line behind. We crossed a field and ran down a long narrow path, still following the robin.

Finally, we got out on to a pavement. In front of us there was a gigantic space covered in tarmac,

with cars parked along it and a lot of people walking around. There were grown-ups on their own, grown-ups with other grown-ups, and grown-ups with children. It was nothing but a common road, but it terrified the three of us. On the other side, there was a line of terraced houses.

'Trrr… tweee-teee-teee…Come! This way! Tweee…' the robin called from where it was sitting on top of a road sign, on the other side of the street.

Chapter 10

Crossing the Road

'We have to be brave now, Orzo,' I said.

'Of course. I'm ready,' he declared from behind me, in a trembling sort of voice.

We hid behind a rubbish bin and made a plan. I tried to keep it simple. If we were spotted, we had to duck under the nearest car straight away.

I told Orzo to keep behind me – we had to stay together. He was shaking like a leaf, but he nodded. Tosca just looked doubtful, as usual.

I waited until nobody was looking our way, then I ran across the pavement with Tosca on my back. When I jumped off it, I nearly fell through a drain cover. I'd been inside a drain before, and the thought of it brought shivers down my spine. I walked carefully around it and let Tosca down. But Orzo hadn't followed us! I put my hand above the kerb and waved, shouting to him to hurry. No one was coming now, why wasn't he crossing? Then I heard a car door slam above us and the engine turn on: the car was about to leave!

I pulled Tosca onto my back. As it drove off, I ducked under the next parked car.

Now we were further away from Orzo. I waved again, to show him where we were. Afraid to be left behind, he rushed out – then panicked and scurried back in again. I decided to climb back up and rescue him myself.

 That's when a group of boys came running down the pavement.

'Hey, I just saw a mouse!' one boy shouted.

Hearing that, Orzo finally decided to dash under the car parked in front of us.

'Where?' another wanted to know.

'It's gone under there!' said the first boy, running to look under the car.

'Let's get some sticks!' said a third boy.

I rushed back under the shelter of our car, and found Orzo zig-zagging from wheel to wheel in a bit of a panic.

Meanwhile, the boys were snapping branches off a shrub in a nearby front garden.

'Quick, Orzo! Now!' I called.

But Orzo couldn't face the open space.

'There it is!' one of the boys said, shoving his stick under the car. Orzo dodged the blow, and with his eyes closed he scurried in our direction and toward the drain that stood between us. I thought he'd fall right into it but he managed to jump over it

nimbly, and landed straight into my arms.

'Well done, Orzo!' I said.

But the boys had seen him scurrying under our car, and starting running towards us with their sticks.

'They're going to kill us!!' Orzo cried.

'Thaaaaat's it,' Tosca croaked.

'Tosca, shut up!' I said. 'Both of you, come with me! Up here!'

I climbed up the tyre and hid behind its metal rim. Three sticks began swinging around the wheel, but not very close to us.

Just when I thought we might be safe, one of the boys peered from the other side of the car and grinned. We climbed up further and squeezed through the suspension spring. The boy poked his stick through the gaps in it, barely missing us.

Just as we thought we had no way out, we heard

a lady's voice:

'What are you doing to my car?! Go away with those sticks!'

The boys laughed and ran off.

The door slammed and the engine was turned on. Orzo jumped on to the ground, and I quickly started climbing down the spring – but I slipped, and Tosca was left stuck behind. I dangled on the spring for a second or two, then fell to the ground. The wheels turned and the car moved forwards a little, then suddenly stopped to wait for the oncoming traffic.

Tosca was still swaying around up there.

'Jump off!' I shouted. But she didn't even try. It was enough to make me scream. I climbed back up the tyre, on to the rim and reached for Tosca's dangling arms.

And then the car began to move.

I grabbed Tosca's hands and pulled at her with all my strength, until we both fell to the ground. The car drove off, leaving us in the middle of the road. With his eyes shut, Orzo scurried to the opposite kerbside and underneath another parked car. Other cars were coming towards us. I pulled Tosca on to my back and dashed for the kerb, right between the wheels of a tandem bike with a man

and a young girl.

'Look, Dad! A running frog! Stop the bike!' the girl said.

I'd already safely dived under the car across the road. I put Tosca down and looked for Orzo, who'd disappeared. When I found him, he was cowering under a tyre.

'That's the worst place to hide!' I said. 'If the car moves it'll squash you!'

I helped him out, and when I turned round I saw the girl's hand pulling Tosca from under the car.

'Look, daddy! Here it is. It was running,' she said.

'Frogs don't run, dear. Now, put it down,' her father said.

'Look. It has a stick on its leg. It must be someone's... Argh! Yuck!' she suddenly shouted. 'It peed on my hand!'

We saw Tosca fall on to the ground. She landed upside down, and wiggled about.

'It's a toad, darling! Take this tissue,' said the girl's father. 'We'll wash your hands when we get to school.'

He kicked Tosca aside with his big foot.

'Disgusting,' he said.

They both climbed back on to their bike, and cycled off.

I rushed to Tosca and pulled her out from under the car.

She was blinking weirdly, but she was conscious.

'Tweee-teee-teee… What took you so loooong… tweee?' the robin called from the front garden opposite us. 'We're nearly there. Tweee.'

We checked the pavement again: it seemed clear. One last effort was needed. We climbed up and ran along its edge. Just as some more people were coming towards us, the robin landed on a hedge and pointed at the garden gate. We ran through, and there it was: a Robin-Red door with a black grille underneath it.

Orzo shot right through the grille like a bullet.

I stopped before the grille: it was going to be a tight squeeze for Tosca.

I turned to thank the robin for his help, but he'd already gone.

I pushed Tosca through one of the slots in the grille.

By the time her big belly finally popped in together with her back legs, I was completely drenched in her squirts. Now it was my turn to see if I could fit through. And that's when the Robin-Red door opened.

Chapter 11

Orzo's Home

A stampede of giant feet fell around me and rushed towards the gate: three children were dashing out of the house. The youngest child, a girl, turned to wait for her mother as she closed the door. And she saw me. I stayed still, hoping she'd ignore me. But she walked back, her eyes gleaming with curiosity. She pointed at me and shouted: 'Mum, wait! Look! A stick with a face!'
But her mother grabbed her arm and pulled her towards the gate.
'Of course, darling. But we don't have time now,' she said. 'You can play with all the sticks you want

at Grannie's house.'

'But Mum, look!'

I quickly slipped down through one of the slots in the grille, and dropped a short distance onto a dusty floor.

'She's gone in!' I heard the girl shout.

'Who's gone in? Where?' her mother asked.

'The stick, Mum!' the girl insisted. 'The stick with the face.'

'Come on, everyone. The car's this way...'

Their voices faded into the distance.

I took a big breath of relief. The light from the grille didn't reach very far at all, so the world ahead of us was very dark and mysterious. But at least it was quiet.

I called Orzo: if this was his home, he could at least guide us through it. But there was no reply. So I put Tosca on my back again, and started walking across the dusty floor, into the unknown.

It soon got so dark that I could hardly see where I was going. I called Orzo again, louder this time. I listened for his reply, but I only heard a screech from overhead. And through a gap in the floorboards, I saw Spritz's blue eyes staring down at us.

I couldn't believe it.

'Of all places, we have to end up at Spritz's home!' I muttered to myself.

'The same caaaaat,' Tosca hurped. 'As I say, we just caaaaan't escape our fate…'

I walked onwards, feeling my way, with no idea where I was going. Eventually we were in total darkness. And, finally, I heard a familiar voice.

'Squee-hee! There you are! Tos-squee and Almond-squee, meet my big brother – Cumin-squee!' Orzo said.

'Cumin. Hi there,' said another squeaky voice, a bit lower than Orzo's.

'Orzo? Where are you?'

'We're here!' Orzo chuckled, touching my arm. 'Right next to you.'

'Oh – there you are…' I said, feeling his fur. 'Hi Cumin… wherever you are.'

'Orzo, why didn't you tell us one of them was a toad?' Cumin asked. 'Mum won't be pleased.'

'She's a nice toad,' Orzo said. 'And she needs help – she's injured. Just don't touch her.'

'Sure I won't. Orzo, you are always bringing problems home. You know toads stink,' Cumin said. 'And they're hideous.'

'Cumin-squee, there's no need to worry. Just roll in the dust and you'll be fine. Squee-hee! Let's go everyone-squee,' Orzo said.

I heard them scurrying off.

'Hey – Orzo!' I called. ''How are we supposed to know where to go?'

'Squee-hee-hee – sorry, I forgot,' he said. 'Here, grab my tail-squee! Mum knows we're coming.'

He guided us through the darkness. Finally, we turned a corner and saw a faint glow coming from a cranny.

'We've arrived,' Orzo said.

A few steps led up to Orzo's home.

'Hello, may I?' I asked politely as I stepped into their den.

'Mummy!' he said. 'Here they are... meet my new friends-squee.'

'For the love of wheat, what is that?' Orzo's mum cried when she saw Tosca, scurrying behind a box and knocking over a few stools on the way. 'A toad? And a big one, at that! Orzo, why did you bring it here?'

'We don't mean to disturb you or stay long,' I said, a little taken aback by her rude welcome. 'But we've had a rough time lately. I'm so glad your son managed to find you again and brought us here.'

'Yes Mum, you should have seen me-squee! I haven't told you what happened yet!' Orzo said.

'Yes, you have some explaining to do,' his mum said. 'I was worried sick about you.'

'Mum, we were trapped in a huge bucket!'

'In a bucket? With these two?'

'Yes! Mum, I tried to scratch the cat and nibble his nose-squee but he grabbed her instead!'

'A cat – for squeaking out loud! Did it catch you?' she said.

'Yes, but I scared it off! You should have seen him. But then he came back,' he said.

'He did?' his mum asked, holding her whiskers.

'Yes! Squee! But then Almond-squee helped us. Me and Tos-squee. When the cat left, she carried Tos-squee all the time... I showed them the way... for a while... but then nobody knew where we were. And then we were attacked by a fox!'

'For husk's sake!' his mum said, incredulous. 'Not a fox, too!'

'Yes! And then we crossed the road...'

'The road? In daytime?' his mum said, sitting down in shock.

As Orzo told her what we'd been doing, I put Tosca down and sat on a cotton spool. I needed some rest, even if I didn't feel all that welcome.

Their home was snug, but very untidy. The floor was littered with husks, nut shells and other waste. Old cobwebs and threads hung from the ceiling. A large table stood in the middle of the den, with

four stools around it. In one corner, behind a curtain made from a torn supermarket bag, there was a pile of cotton wool, straws and tatters that seemed to be their bed. A chipped coffee cup and a thimble were collecting water from a dripping pipe. Even my old home was neat compared to this place! I wondered how they could live in such a mess. Tosca sat on top of an old die and stretched her leg.

'Excuse me,' Orzo's mum said to Tosca. 'Please don't sit there. Or anywhere. You two, come along with me.'

She led us behind another curtain – this one was a dirty piece of muslin – and into a smaller, darker area which looked like a storage space for discarded objects.

'I'll be back,' she said, leaving us there.

She sharply closed the curtain, and went to talk to her children.

'Orzo, why did you rescue those two?' I heard her whispering. 'One of them looks like a human, of

all things! And a toad! A vile, poisonous toad!'

'Mum, they don't know how to get home-squee.'

'Toads are horrible,' said Cumin.

'We need to get rid of them,' his mother said. 'A toad in my house…'

'What about the little weird human? Are you sure she's safe, Orzo?' Cumin added.

'Humans are sly,' his mother answered. 'They offer you food to kill you! Remember what your poor dad used to say about humans:

>*The only time they give you bread*
>*It's in a trap to kill you dead.*

We don't want any problems, kids. These two don't belong with us. I'll talk to them.'

I stopped listening and walked back to Tosca. I checked the stick splint around her leg, and tightened the knots.

'How are you?' I asked her.

Tosca blinked slowly. Before she answered, I interrupted her.

'No, Tosca! We aren't going to die,' I said. 'Here or anywhere else. We'll find our home – one way or another. And you'll cheer up again.'

I lay down on a piece of rag, exhausted. It was nice to rest in a safe place for a change. But were we really safe? The mice didn't seem to want us there. I fell asleep wondering how long we could stay out of danger, and where else we could go.

Chapter 12

A Cosy Dungeon

I felt someone gently shaking me out of my sleep.
It was Orzo.

'Mum said you can stay tonight if you wash. But
we can't keep Tos-squee here,' he said.

'Orzo, she can't go anywhere!' I said. 'Not until
her leg is better. I'll talk to her.'

'You have to wash first. Mum says you stink of
toad-squee. Go over there, where it drains,' he said
pointing to a recess in the corner where the
wooden floor sloped toward a hole. I saw that he'd
put the thimble next to me. It was filled to the
brim with clean water.

'OK. Thanks for the water… I'll need more shortly,' I said.

I helped Tosca over to the corner and emptied the washbowl over her, moistening her dry skin. She croaked and smacked her lips.

'The water was for you, not her-squee,' Orzo said.

I gave him back the bucket and asked for more.

Moments later, his mother came back with it full. But she wasn't happy.

'We can't keep toads in our house,' she said. 'They pee all over the place. It's disgusting. And dangerous.'

'I'll take care of it if there's an accident. I promise.'

'And who'll take care of the smell?'

'I will,' I said. 'We won't overstay our welcome.' I took the thimble to wash myself. I saw her looking at my dress. It wasn't just dirty: it was torn beyond repair.

'You can't wear that old rag any more. Take it off,' she said.

She left the room, then quickly came back with some old pieces of fabric. I took two long strips of yellow cotton and tied one around my chest and one around my waist, making myself a simple top and a miniskirt. She seemed pleased with how quickly I arranged my new dress, and with the result.

'Thank you so much,' I said. 'This is perfect. And very comfortable too.'

She was still staring at me.

She seemed interested in my leafy appearance.

'My name's Almondine,' I said, offering my hand. 'Can I ask yours?'

She hesitated, as if having to reveal a secret. Then she gave me her chubby pink fingers and told me her name was Granola. But she frowned at Tosca, who was licking her wet lips.

'Your hospitality means a lot to me. And to my friend Tosca, too,' I said, before Granola had a chance to say anything else about her dislike of toads. 'Look at her leg; she's injured. She needs time to recover.'

Granola gave Tosca a compassionate look. Then she turned to me again.

'Use this for her,' she said, handing me another piece of cloth. 'And make sure she stays dry! Then come through. It's time for dinner.'

Granola left.

'I'm sorry, Tosca, but you'll have to wear this,' I said.

I doubled up the cloth and wrapped it around her lower body.

'Ha ha!' I chortled. 'It looks like you're wearing a nappy! Like a baby.'

The toad didn't care what she looked like.

Moments later we were all sitting at the table, the mice all together at one end, Tosca and I at quite a distance. Granola opened a little pouch and

handed five grains of rice to each of us. The mice quivered their whiskers three times, rubbed their ears, then pointed their noses up while chattering their teeth. *It must be their pre-meal ritual*, I thought. Then they quickly nibbled up their grains of rice, each one of them concluding their feast with a forceful 'Burp!'

Granola noticed that Tosca and I weren't touching our food.

'We don't want to be rude,' I said. 'But we... we can't really eat this food. Would you happen to have any insects for Tosca?'

'Yes!' Orzo shouted. 'Plenty!'

He ran out of the room, then came back and dropped a couple of dead flies on the table in front of Tosca.

'The underfloor's full of these,' he said.

Tosca snatched one with her tongue and chewed it slowly.

'Fly eaters!' Granola said. 'At my table!'

'And what do you eat?' asked Cumin suspiciously.

'Oh, just earth, for me, please,' I said. 'If there is any available.'

'Surely you can't eat that,' Cumin said.

'She does!' Orzo chuckled. 'I've seen her!'

'And an earth eater!' Granola said to herself, holding her forehead.

'Well, there's plenty of earth down in the cellar!' Cumin said. He still didn't believe it.

'I'll get a spade,' said Orzo, grabbing a little shard of wood.

'I want to see this,' Cumin sniggered.

When Orzo offered me his find, I ate it politely.

'She really does eat earth!' Cumin, said, delighted.

'I told you,' said Orzo.

The two young mice laughed together.

Granola was actually very kind, and she began to warm to us. So that night wasn't the only one that we were allowed to stay.

In the end, it was us who wanted to leave.

Chapter 13

Missing Home

I'm not sure how many days went by. We couldn't see the sun, so we relied on the light from the humans' house, shining down on us through a crack. We spent most of our time in the dark and my eyes began to adapt to the gloomy place they called home.

The mouse family often argued, and knocked things about while they did. They always seemed to be on edge. Maybe animals like mice can't help being frightened most of the time. But I started to get a bit tired of all the chaos.

I wanted to help. I started by cleaning and tidying

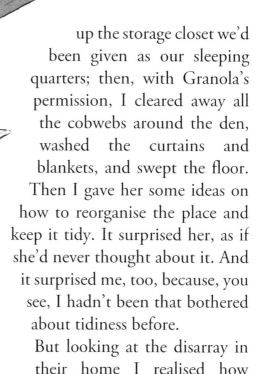

up the storage closet we'd been given as our sleeping quarters; then, with Granola's permission, I cleared away all the cobwebs around the den, washed the curtains and blankets, and swept the floor. Then I gave her some ideas on how to reorganise the place and keep it tidy. It surprised her, as if she'd never thought about it. And it surprised me, too, because, you see, I hadn't been that bothered about tidiness before.

But looking at the disarray in their home I realised how confusing and annoying it was to live like that. Over time, their living quarters began to feel more spacious and comfortable. And, miraculously, they didn't argue quite so much as they did before.

Granola then asked me if I could help make a dress for her, too. I didn't know how to sew, but I was quite good at making knots. So I improvised with a few rags from her den and made her a nice, colourful dress. She was very happy with it, and was eager to learn more. When I'd taught her how to tie things together, Granola was finally able to make good use of all the pieces of fabric they had collected, decorating their home and making many more dresses for herself. I'd become her stylist!

I intrigued the young mice, too, when I showed them what certain objects they'd stolen from the humans were meant for. We also adapted some into useful tools for their simple needs.

I wasn't an expert at things like this, but I used my imagination, which wasn't bad, compared with that of a mouse.

So, before too long, they were eating sweet, warm porridge served with a spoon, in a bowl, on a clean, white tablecloth.

Tosca kept wearing her nappy, so they didn't mind her any more. And, over time, she was becoming able to move her leg a bit.

The mice fetched food for us every day from the

dark labyrinth of the underfloor, and we spent the evenings telling stories and getting to know each other better.

After dinner I heard Granola tucking her two children in bed and giving them a loving kiss. It hurt, because it reminded me of Alma: I missed her and my home so much. Why hadn't I appreciated it? What had I been thinking?

One night I was lying in bed, unable to sleep because of these thoughts, and wondering what we should do next.

Tosca had already settled down for the night in a water-filled saucer, which was perfect for her aching joints and delicate skin.

I glanced over at her, and she opened her eyes.

'Did I wake you up?' I said.

She looked at me and smiled.

'Thaaank you, Almondine,' she replied.

'Why are you thanking me, all of a sudden?'

'Nobody ever did whaaat you did for me. Hurp. Not even my old Maaaaarioad.'

'Who?'

'Maaaaarioad. Aaarfter we had eggs together, he left me,' she said.

A tear fell from her eye. For the first time since I'd met her, she was showing some emotion.

'I'm sorry to hear that, Tosca,' I said. 'It must have been hard to be on your own.'

'Then my eggs haaaaatched,' Tosca nodded, 'and all my tadpoles left me. Too. And after thaaat day, I was just aaanother toad: food for herons and snaaakes, a toy for humans and caaaaats, a taaarget for caaaaars. Worthless. A useless nothing. Hurp.'

'Don't say that, Tosca. Your life is as valuable as any other.'

'You aaare special, Almondine. You aaare a very good person.'

I shook my head. 'I wouldn't be here now if I was. I often argued with my mum. And now I miss her.'

'Aaaand I'm sure she is missing you too. Hurp.'

'She probably is.'

'And now we're stuck down here till the daaaaay

we die. Hurp.'

'No, Tosca. We won't die here. I'm going to see my mum again. And you… you'll see your tadpoles again, too.'

'They won't be tadpoles aaaaany more.'

'It doesn't matter. We'll work out a plan, and we'll leave this place soon.'

But we still had a problem to deal with outside the mice's den.

And the problem was called Spritz.

Chapter 14

Dangerous Plan

Living in the dark wasn't good for me at all. Quite like my skin, the leaves on my head and body became very pale and they began to wither. I was losing my appetite and I often felt dizzy.

One evening I broke the news that it was time for us to leave.

'But you don't have to! You're like family now!' was Granola's reaction.

She asked why we wanted to leave.

The reason was clear: we didn't belong there.

But how we were going to escape with Spritz

constantly patrolling the house was another matter.

'The cat is always locked in the house at night,' said Cumin. 'And they let him out first thing in the morning.'

'That's why they brought it here, months ago!' said Granola. 'Since they took poor old Dad... They think it will catch the rest of us! Oh, how I miss the days when we could get into their home at night...'

'It's dangerous leaving at night,' I said. 'Tosca, what do you think?'

'Hurp. Whaaatever.'

'Tosca, we are doing this together!' I said.

'But where do you waaaaant to go?'

Actually, she was right. How would we know where to go, anyway? We needed a guide. I immediately thought of the robin: if I could talk to him again, maybe he'd be able to show me where my home was. If Spritz lived here, it couldn't be too far. But what about Tosca? The robin couldn't help her.

'We need somebody who has an overview of the

area,' I said. 'Someone who can take us with them to look around.'

'What about Broona?' Orzo asked.

'Yes, that's right,' said Cumin, 'Broona can help! Or can she? I can never understand a single thing she says.'

'Me neither,' chuckled Orzo. 'But she has got wings-squee!'

'And no brain. Anyway, she's hardly ever around.'

'Spritz keeps everyone away,' sighed Granola.

'Hang on,' I said.

'Who is Broona?'

'She's a wood pigeon,' said Cumin. 'Broona comes for her bath in our back garden every morning. We can see her through a hole at the end of the house. But it's dangerous.'

The next day, I woke up early and together with Cumin and Orzo we went to the hole that looked out on their lawn.

There was a stone bird bath on a tall pedestal under a bay tree. We waited, and watched Broona arrive and splash around in it, washing her feathers. Against my friends' advice, I rushed out of the hole and ran into the tall grass, waving to attract the bird's attention.

'Broona!' I called. 'I need to talk to you!'
'Broo!' she said, raising her head, alarmed.
'Broona, I'm here...' I shouted, trying to jump up above the grass.

I began to explain our dire situation, hoping for an encouraging reply from her. But I soon realised that Broona couldn't see me in the overgrown lawn, and could hardly hear my voice. She looked around for a while, repeating the same call; then, abruptly, she took off. A moment later, I

saw Spritz lazily sidling into the garden and heading towards the little hole in the wall. I ran back as fast as I could, but he saw me coming. He bounded towards me but I managed to slip back inside, just in time.

The two mice hugged me. They were shaking.

'I told you it's dangerous!' Cumin cried.

'Almond-squee, that was so cool!' said Orzo and then pulled a funny face at Spritz who was intently watching us through the narrow hole.

I was not resigned. It'd just be a matter of choosing the right timing. My real problem was the wood pigeon. How was I going to talk to Broona if she couldn't even see me? It didn't help that I looked a bit like a weed myself. I needed to get closer to her, where she couldn't miss me, and where I could talk her into helping us.

I studied the surroundings: the garden, the bird bath, the bay tree.

Then I had an idea.

Chapter 15

Setting out for Home

Early next morning, I hugged Granola and thanked her for their hospitality. She was sad that we were leaving, and apologised for being rude when she first met us, especially to Tosca.

Their home looked very different now. Granola's latest frock was very pretty, and even Orzo and Cumin were wearing neat new clothes. I was proud of having helped them.

Tosca had regained some strength in her leg but she still wasn't able to hop properly. Nonetheless she seemed relieved she could now lose her nappy. And so, we said goodbye to Granola, and followed

Orzo and Cumin down the dark passages that led to the garden hole.

When we arrived there, I hugged the two mice one last time, and we squeezed out of the hole. It was just before dawn, and we needed to act quickly for our plan to work. We plunged into the deep grass and walked onwards.

After a while, we reached the bay tree.

I knew I could only talk to Broona if she could see me on the bird bath. The basin was impossible to reach from underneath, so I planned on jumping onto it from an overhanging branch.

But first, I had to get up there.

Luckily, most of the bay tree's trunk was covered in ivy, which helped me hold onto it. But climbing was difficult with Tosca on my back. When I reached the branch over the bird bath, my arms and legs were trembling with the effort. There was no time to waste, though: the sun was already beginning to glow through the foliage.

We crawled to the point directly above the bird bath. It was going to be a big, scary jump.

'Tosca, if Spritz comes out you'll be safe up here,' I said. 'I'll see if I can get Broona to rescue you. But if I can't, or if anything else happens to me, just wait here until evening, when Spritz goes back inside. Then jump into the bird bath and find your way back to the mice. Can you do that?'

'Hurp,' was her only answer.

With my heart in my mouth, I held my nose and jumped down into the bird bath.

I hit the water with a big splash, then swam toward the edge where I could touch the bottom with my feet. As I waited for the wood pigeon, waist-high in the water, I scanned the trees around me.

'Where is she?' I wondered. 'She should be here by now.'

Spritz was sitting at one of the upstairs windows, his blue eyes gazing in my direction. I slowly lowered myself into the water, hoping he hadn't seen me. When I checked again, he'd gone.

Then I heard a flutter of wings behind me. I turned to see that Broona had finally landed on the edge of the bowl.

'Broona!' I whispered. 'Hello, Broona... do you remember me?'

'Broo!'

'Broo to you... we need help.'

'Broo are you?' she asked, pecking at one of the

leaves on my head.

'Ouch! Don't do that… Please… I'm Almondine. And my friend up there is Tosca,' I said, pointing to the tree above. 'We need you to help us.'

'Broorry?'

Communication wasn't going to be easy. I tried another tack.

'Can I… broo… on top of your broo? You… then… broo us away. Together. On your broo. Makes sense? Do you under-broo me?'

She stared at me, silently.

'Oh, please, I will broo any broo for you… if you broo this small broo for us,' I said, hoping to be

understood in her language. Broona still didn't
say anything. She just took off from the bird bath
and flew into a tree in the next garden.

'Not again. Come back!' I cried.

How stupid I'd been, I thought. She was never
going to help us.

Then, seconds later, Spritz jumped on to the bird
bath in her place.

Chapter 16

Team

Tosca was right: we were all going to die after all, and I was going to be first.

Spritz wanted to grab me, but he didn't want to get wet. So he started to walk around the edge of the bird bath. His stare was terrifying. I backed away, but he was faster than me.

Then, suddenly, something slammed on to his face. It was Tosca! Now she was grasping his head. He thrashed about, until he slipped and fell off on to the grass.

I looked over the rim and saw Spritz a few paces away, licking his paws and cleaning his eyes. Tosca was upside down, wriggling her legs and trying to roll back onto her feet.

Without thinking twice, I jumped off the bird bath and on to the grass, which helped soften my landing.

I ran up to Tosca, pulled her on to my back and pushed into the grass. I didn't have a clue where I was heading, but I ran as fast as I could, occasionally turning back to check what Spritz was doing. Surely he could see the grass shaking as we passed? I remembered how fast he could run, and I just managed to squeeze under a nearby shed as he pounced.

He kept groping under the shed floor with his

paw, but he couldn't reach us. After trying for a while, he gave up and to our relief, he went away. When I peered out, I saw him already at the end of the garden, staring at the hole in the wall of the house where we'd squeezed out. He knew where we'd come from and must have smelt the young mice inside. His tail was wagging slowly, and I prayed that Orzo and Cumin would stay safe.

I turned to Tosca and held her hands.

'Tosca, you saved me.'

'You saaaaved me too. Hurp.'

I hugged her.

I could feel my stress ebbing away.

'Friends,' I said.

'Friends,' she replied, curling her long, fat lips upwards.

'We're a team. And we will not be defeated!' I stated with conviction.

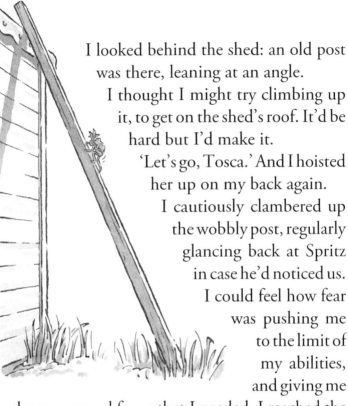

I looked behind the shed: an old post was there, leaning at an angle.

I thought I might try climbing up it, to get on the shed's roof. It'd be hard but I'd make it.

'Let's go, Tosca.' And I hoisted her up on my back again.

I cautiously clambered up the wobbly post, regularly glancing back at Spritz in case he'd noticed us. I could feel how fear was pushing me to the limit of my abilities, and giving me the energy and focus that I needed. I reached the top of the post, and we got on to the roof of the shed. My heart was still pounding, but I hoped we were out of his reach now.

Looking around, I saw Broona resting on a tree next door. She must have seen us escape.

I waved, encouraging her to come to us. But she didn't move from her branch, and kept cocking her head, as if puzzled. I wasn't going to give up on our only hope. One of the branches of Broona's

tree was touching the roof of the shed.
I thought I'd use it as a bridge to get to Broona.

With Tosca on my back again, I stepped on to it
and made my way towards her, carefully holding
on with both hands and feet.

She seemed to be waiting for us. With each
cautious step, I was getting closer to Broona, close
enough to have another conversation with her.

Then, suddenly, a squirrel jumped on to the branch, barring the way and making the branch shake so much that we nearly went tumbling to the ground.

'Who said you could cross the line?!' he squeaked with a raspy voice. 'This is my territory! Introduce yourselves!'

Before I could answer, I noticed that Broona had gone. And, with her, our only hope of finding our way home.

Chapter 17

Sergeant Spencer

'Look at me when I talk to you!' The squirrel insisted. 'Stand up and answer me! Or I'll throw you off! No Wingless Being can walk these branches without my consent!'

With all my hopes shattered, I didn't even try to answer him at first. I simply let Tosca slip off my back and stood up.

'We'll leave now,' I said.

Tosca crouched next to me on the branch, and only then did the squirrel realise that we were actually two creatures.

He couldn't believe his big, black eyes.

'This can't be!' he said. Then he bowed to us. 'Forgive me, your majesty,' he said, solemnly. 'I never thought I'd ever meet a real Queenut.'

I looked at Tosca. She was as confused as me. 'And on one of my trees!' he continued. 'Today is the best day of my life. I'm at your service, your majesty. To what do I owe the honour?'

I looked at Tosca and she raised one of her knobbly eyebrows. If we let the squirrel believe that I was this queen of his, maybe he'd help us. 'My friend, Tosca, needs to return home,' I said in a grave voice.

'The toad?' he asked, surprised.

'Her name is Tosca,' I said, sternly.

'Of course your majesty – of course. Ready to serve,' the squirrel replied, lowering his head.

'You are a good squirrel,' I declared.

'Spencer, your majesty,' he said, proudly perking up his tail. 'Sergeant Sorrel Spencer.'

'Thank you, Sergeant Spencer. I need one moment with my friend, then it will be your duty to escort her home safely.'

I turned to Tosca while Spencer waited patiently for his next order.

'Tosca, we're so lucky, I whispered to her. 'This is your chance!'

'Whaaaaat about you? Hurp.'

'I'll find my way, don't worry. Now, go. And try to cheer up!'

'I'll miss you,' Tosca said, her eyes wet.

'I'll miss you too, Tosca,' I said, hugging her. She gently stroked one of my leaves.

'I'll remember you aaand the courage you gaaaave me for the rest of my daaaaays,' she said. '...Hurp.'

'I'll remember you, too,' I said. 'And good luck finding your children again.'

'You haaave love in your heart. It haaas changed my destiny. And it will change yours, too.'

We hugged again, and Tosca hopped off towards Spencer. Then she turned to me.

'Don't be afraaaid of your destiny,' she said.

There was surprising wisdom in Tosca's last words. I hadn't imagined she had it in her. Maybe her sombre attitude had misled me: she was thoughtful and sensitive after all. Perhaps too much so. Maybe that was what made her seem a little weird.

I watched her describing her home pond to Spencer, who immediately knew which direction to take. She got on to his back, and he held her comfortably tight against his body with his furry tail. Then he sprang off. In a blink, they'd disappeared from view. The swishing of leaves as they jumped from branch to branch showed the direction they were taking – and then all the trees were still, and they were gone.

I was happy for Tosca, and I imagined her happy too, surrounded by her toad children.

I sighed and looked down. I could see the shed roof we'd come from, and the garden we'd left behind just minutes ago.

And I could see Spritz, staring up at me.

Chapter 18

Bumpy Flight

I kept still. Spritz started to walk towards the shed, his eyes fixed on me. I scanned every branch for Broona, and called for her with all my might.
'Brooo-na! Brooo-na!'
Hearing my cries, Spritz paused, then disappeared behind a shrub near the fence.
I knew I had to get away from this place. I walked further up the branch, but the further I went, the thinner and more wobbly it became. My legs started to tremble. I lost my balance, and fell into the garden next door.
I came round in the shade of a lavender bush.

I was a bit bruised. I rubbed my head and tried to hide.

And there, to my relief, I saw Broona, gingerly waddling towards me.

'Broona! Thank goodness you are still here!' I said.

'Broo,' she replied.

I remembered how difficult our last conversation had been.

'Broona, thank you for… brooing here,' I began. 'I need your help.'

'Broo.'

I left the bush and inched closer, careful not to scare her off.

'I need to get out of here. Can you take me with you?' I asked, pointing first to myself, and then to her back.

'Broo? Broo you?' she replied, in a kind of questioning tone.

'Yes!' I said. 'Me… on top of you… then we fly.' I gestured to make myself clear. Broona was looking at my waving arms and cocked her head.

'Me and you… broo! In the sky! Looking for my home… I mean, me brooing for my broo…' I improvised. 'Please, I will do anything you want… any broo you broo. Please.'

Somehow, it seemed to work.

'Broo!' Broona nodded. 'Broona will broo you to your broo!'

She hopped closer, briefly spreading her wings.

'But will you broo a broo for Broona?' she asked. I didn't know exactly what this meant, but it couldn't be anything too hard.

'Yes, I will broo anything for you,' I told her.

She squatted, seemingly inviting me to climb up. Then, when I was just about to, she suddenly grabbed my arm with her beak, flapped her wings and took off.

I wondered what had got into her. Her beak pinched my skin with a stinging pain. I looked back at where we'd been standing and I saw Spritz in our place, looking disappointed as he watched us leaving.

Broona had just saved me from his claws!

I clenched my teeth and tried to resist the pain, thankful for what she'd done for me. We flew higher and higher, and I soon began to appreciate how tightly she was holding me, as I didn't want

to drop from that distance.

But as I looked at the gardens, roofs and streets that were zipping along below me, I had a horrible feeling that we were flying back to where I'd come from.

'No, Broona, not this way!' I shouted. 'Turn back!'

She flew over the railway track where I'd sheltered with Tosca and Orzo, then over the tunnel and along the road. She was taking me further and further back.

'No, Broona, please!' I insisted. 'You're going the wrong way!'

But she didn't listen.

Finally, the flapping of her wings grew gentler, and we descended towards a quiet railway station. We landed on a big, untidy nest resting on the branches of a tree that overhung the end of the

platform. She dropped me on the dirty straw, right next to a big wood pigeon chick who took up almost the whole nest.

'Chicobroo doesn't broo,' Broona said. 'Can you broo him to broo?'

The chick was staring back at me, as if terrified by my presence.

'Broo him out of my broo!' she said. 'You are very broo. Then I'll broo your broo.'

And with that, Broona was off.

I checked below: it was a sheer drop. There was no way out of this grimy nest.

I couldn't believe my bad luck.

Minutes earlier I'd been a squirrel's queen: now I was a pigeon's prisoner.

Chapter 19

Chicobroo

The sooner I could make this bird leave his nest, it seemed, the sooner Broona would come back and rescue me. Anyway, I hoped that was the idea, because she couldn't just abandon me there.

Either way, I had no choice but to see what I could do to get him to fly.

I looked at Chicobroo again. He was almost fully grown. In fact he was so big that I had to stand right at the edge of the nest, and any movement he made could knock me out of it.

I tried to ignore what my bare feet where standing on. The floor of the nest was covered in a grimy white crust. And Chicobroo's ruffled breast was comfortably nestled on it.

'What are you brooing here?' he asked timidly, staring at me with one eye.

'Good question. I promised your mother that I'd do anything she asked if she took me home, and she brought me here. Come on, Chicobroo. The sooner you leave this ghastly place, the sooner I can get home.'

Chicobroo lowered his head and settled even more deeply into the nest. He looked at me again, and there was terror in his eyes.

'I'm not brooing anywhere,' he said.

'Why are you so scared? You're big and strong!' I patted one of his wings but he shifted away, as if he was afraid of being touched.

'Can I see?' I asked.

He didn't say anything, so I carefully lifted one of his wings and spread it out to its full glory.

'Look at this! It's so beautiful and perfect. Can I see the other one?' I asked, and he opened it for me. I was genuinely impressed. 'They are so gorgeous! I wish I had a pair of these, too.'

And I was being honest. You see, I really would have liked wings like that.

He closed them and looked away.

'I can't,' he said, miserably.

'Yes, yes, yes you can!' I said. 'Like I say, you're big and strong. Let's do this.'

I was feeling a bit impatient, so I tried to push him off the edge.

'Off you go! C'mon! Just flap your wings up and down. You're made to fly!'

'Broo off me!' he said.

'No. You're the one who should broo off!' I said, struggling to shift his weight.

'Broo off me!!' he said again, louder this time.

'No, you broo off!!' I repeated, still shoving his rear. 'Broo off! C'mon, you! Broo! Off you broo!!'

I didn't even know what I was saying any more when he suddenly turned and pecked me on the head. I fell backwards, but managed to land inside the nest.

As I looked up, he turned away, sulkily. My head hurt. I was so furious, I could have strangled him.

'I'm just trying to help you! Don't you get it?' I shouted to him, disappointed. Then I heard him sniffle. 'Chicobroo?' I said, a bit worried now. 'What's the matter?' 'I broot you!' he sobbed. 'You are just like Mum… I broo you all! I broo her! I broo my brothers! Nobody broos me! No-broo-body!' This sudden anger and sadness stunned me.

'Come on, now,' I said. 'Why do you hate them so much? What have they done to you?'

'Everyone's always broolling me. Brooce and Brooto… those broollies… broolling me all the time… they brooed all my food… brooshd me around…' he sobbed.

'And my mum too, brooing me and brooing me…' he went on in a cracked voice. 'She brooed me too… and now you!'

'Sorry, Chicobroo, I didn't realise...' I said, sitting down next to him. The poor chick was very upset, and now he told me why.

He'd been the smallest of three brothers, and had been ignored, pushed around and left to starve since he was born. When the time came to take off, he just didn't have the confidence. Broona had tried to hustle him out of the nest, and he'd had a scuffle with her. Both ended up feeling annoyed with each other.

As I listened to how he had been mistreated, I began to feel sorry for him.

I remembered how I'd sometimes hated my mum for exactly the opposite reasons. I'd have felt horrible if Alma had wanted to get rid of me, instead of wanting to keep me safe and protected! Broona's intentions may have been good, but the way she put them into practice was too harsh for poor Chicobroo. He was broken, and he needed help. I forgot about my quest and decided to see what I could do for him.

I thought that maybe all he yearned for was someone gentle with him and just some honest encouragement. So I tried to be nice to him and appreciate what made him truly special and beautiful to me. As I stroked his glossy plumage, he started to relax and listened to my words as if they were filling a dark void inside his heart. And that felt pleasant to me too.

We watched three beautiful sunsets together as I comforted him and tried to give him strength. But by the time the third one came round, I ran out of

things to say. And he still wouldn't budge.

'Chico, please, I beg you. We won't go anywhere if you keep looking down with that face. Stop staring at the track like that and look up at the sky,' I said to him, exhausted.

'I'll end up like… like him,' he muttered.

'Like who?'

'My uncle… He's still down there.'

'Oh! Where?' I said. 'What happened to him?'

'He… he… fell. Down there… he was hit. But I don't want to broo about it,' he shivered, fearfully.

I stroked Chico to try and comfort him. But it all seemed so futile. With memories like this, how could he ever take off?

Chapter 20

Falling into Space

'First of all, you must only think about good things,' I said.

Chicobroo's stomach rumbled.

'I'm so broongry!' he complained.

'Me too,' I said.

Of course, why hadn't I thought of it! I could use his hunger to get him off the nest! I told him what kind of food can be found in parks, streets and gardens. I told him about bird feeders, bird baths and plants loaded with berries and fruit. It was a question of starving to death in his nest, I said, or flying off and finding all kinds of delicious food.

Soon, he stopped looking at the railway tracks and shifted his gaze to the trees and surrounding homes. His appetite was guiding his imagination. When the rising sun woke me up on the fourth day, he'd gone.

I immediately checked he had not fallen and crashed down below and to my relief, it was clear he had taken off.

'Well done, Chicobroo!' I shouted. "Go to Broona – tell her you've left the nest! Ask her to come and get me! Chicobroo… Chicobroo…!'

After calling him several times, my enthusiasm began to wane.

Had Chicobroo and Broona both abandoned me?

I hoped that nothing happened to them.

I waited the whole day. Nothing. I could hardly sleep that night.

Next morning, I was exhausted – but I wasn't going to give up and die there. I made a decision. I was going to climb under the nest and slide down the vertical branch supporting it. It was very risky. The bark was so smooth, and the branches so big, that I could easily lose my grip and fall. But another day in the nest without food or water would have been the end of me. I worked out that if I could slide down to the next side branch, maybe I could make my way down to the ground. If I was going to die, at least I'd die trying.

With my fingers firmly clasping the twigs of the nest, I slowly climbed over the edge.

As soon as I was hanging over the deep drop, the smallest gust of wind became a threat.

I forced myself not to look down, and to stay focused on my hands. As I lowered myself further below the nest, I had to let my feet dangle as they kept slipping. Then I swung, hand over hand, towards the branch. But just as I got close to it, I

made the mistake of looking down, and I panicked. I could reach it with just a few more swings, but my elbows were trembling. I was paralysed by fear.

Then I felt the nest above me shake, and I nearly lost my grip. 'Broo? What are you brooing down there?' asked Chicobroo, while staring down at me over the edge. 'Look what I've brooed! It's a piece of broo for you!'

He offered me part of a crisp with his beak.
'Chicobroo, where have you been all this time!?'
I shouted.
'I broo off!' he said, dropping his crisp. 'I did it!!
And found lots of broo! Want to broo some?'
'Chico, I'm stuck! I don't want any *broo* now!' I
said, holding on for dear life.
'I can broo you something else. I can broo
anywhere I want to! Brook at me! I can
broo! And it feels so broooo!!'
He took off and flew around the
tree, showing me how agile and
confident he'd become.

'Chicobroo, come back, please!' I begged.
He came back and landed in the nest again.
'All those broo-givers out there!' he continued.
'The brhoomans. Dropping broo everywhere.
And the gardens… I've already brooed
everywhere. And I saw my broothers, broo! They

couldn't broo it when they brooed me.'

'Chicobroo, I need help!'

'I still haven't brooed my mum, though. Did she broo back?'

'Please, Chico, listen to me!!'

'Why are you brooing down there?'

'Because I can't move! Can't you see? I'm stuck!'

He pondered this for a moment, then started to repeat some of the reassuring things I'd been telling him these past few days.

'Don't listen to your brooes... You need to broo in yourself...' he recited, with his eyes closed.

'No, Chicobroo! I don't need comforting. I need you to pick me up!'

'Trust me, I really do broo in you... You are strong and broo, and with your breootiful wings...'

'But I don't have wings!' I shouted.

'You don't? Then what are all those brooers for?'

'They aren't feathers! They're leaves… Chico! I'm slipping!!'

I tried to adjust my grip one last time, but I couldn't hold on. I fell.

I could feel my heart beating in my throat as I saw the nest quickly zooming away from me and Chicobroo's puzzled look as he watched me fall. If I were to hit the concrete below, I knew I'd die. And then everything went black.

Chapter 21

Track Failure

Next thing I knew, I was waking up on the railway platform, under the tree I'd fallen from. I must have fainted. But how had I survived the fall?

'Why did you broo off?' I heard a familiar voice asking me.

I turned and saw Chicobroo hopping off a bench. 'Was that you? Did you just save me?' I asked him, rubbing my head.

'I brooed you onto my back before you brooed to the ground. You made me brool and broomble too!' he said.

'Chico!' I cried, hugging him with all my might.

'Aooch…' he coughed. 'You're brooing my neck!'
'Sorry,' I said releasing him from my over-enthusiastic embrace.

Down the platform, people were starting to arrive, and some were walking in our direction. We hid underneath the bench, near the wall of the station.
'Chico, I have a favour to ask of you,' I whispered. 'I can see how happy you are that you can fly…'
'I do. I broo it! Broo at me!' he said excitedly, and took off.
'Come back!' I shouted, worried that he'd leave me again.
He came back.
'You see!' he said. 'I want to broo you so much for brooing me…'

'Listen, Chico. Stay here and hear me out. I need to find my way home. So I want you to fly me over this neighbourhood.'

He cocked his head a few times, staring at me with one eye.

'If you let me sit on your back, you can take me up with you. I don't weigh too much.'

He didn't look convinced.

'Me, brooing you on my broo? I don't think I can broo it.'

'Can we just try, Chico? Please. You've been so brave already. You're free now, but I have no idea where I am. Please, help me find my home.'

Chicobroo started looking around. He seemed to be weighing up my plea, but was still unsure if he could offer any help. He began to walk away.

'Please, Chico. Don't leave me…'

My voice broke, and my eyes filled with tears.

Chicobroo hopped back.

'Alright. Let's broo it,' he said.

'Thank you, Chico. Thank you so much,' I said, relieved.

He settled down, and I climbed on to his back. When he stood up, his legs trembled, and he lurched a bit before he was able to stop and focus on the platform. I gently hugged his neck.

He started running and flapping his wings very hard. We took off, but as we crossed the railway track, he lost control.

He swerved, twisted and zigzagged, then dropped sharply, right in the middle of the opposite railway track.

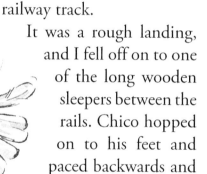

It was a rough landing, and I fell off on to one of the long wooden sleepers between the rails. Chico hopped on to his feet and paced backwards and forwards, frightened.

'I'm so broo… I can't… it's too broo…' he said.

He took off.

'No Chico… come back…' I sighed, knowing he wouldn't come back for a long time – if ever.

A train could arrive at any time. I looked to one side: the railway tracks converged towards a

tunnel. I turned the other way, and had a start when I saw some pigeon feathers scattered between the rails.

This was what had become of Chico's uncle, the one who'd fallen.

Chico must have seen the remains when he was flying, and the sight had made him panic again.

Where was I to go now?

I couldn't imagine a worse place to be trapped: between two huge metal walls, surrounded by crushed stones, and maybe about to be run over by a train.

People were crowding along both platforms. Maybe someone would take pity on me, and help.

I waved my arms, hoping one of them would notice. I called for help, but it was no use. Everyone seemed occupied by a phone, or a newspaper, or by just watching out for the next train. Nobody looked down at me. Anyway, I probably looked more like a waving twig than a little person in need.

Then there was an unbelievably loud noise, and the huge, dark underside of a train suddenly rolled along the tracks and glided over me, turning the day into night and bringing a hurricane with it. I spun over the gravel together with cigarettes, leaves and debris of all kinds, until I fell into a nook between the stones.

The train stopped. Through a long, illuminated slit, I saw feet climbing on and off it. I tried to stand up, but my back hurt. The world was spinning. I collapsed, and everything went dark once again.

Chapter 22

Shelter from the Storm

I'm not sure how long I lay there, unconscious. Thunder woke me up, and I saw that the sky had turned leaden grey. The platforms were empty.

I stood up with difficulty. I was weak, and my body was sore. Where could I go?

First of all, I had to get off the tracks. But how? They were impossible to cross, and too high for me to climb.

Then I noticed, not too far away, several bolts jutting out from a long slab of steel where one part of the track joined the next. I could climb them like the rungs of a ladder, and reach the other side.

I crawled over the gravel towards the joint. The stones were like boulders to me.

The sky was darkening quickly, and heavy drops of rain began to burst around me. I had to rush, as a big storm was about to start.

When I arrived at the joint, I hurriedly climbed up the bolts to get to the top. I could feel the track trembling under me: another train was coming, but it must have still been some way off, as I couldn't see it yet. The rain was getting harder, and I worried that the metal would soon be too slippery to climb.

I pressed on, determined to cross before the train arrived. But haste was clouding my judgment. When I finally got on to the wet, steel surface of

the top of the track, I saw the train coming towards me at full speed.

I didn't have time to climb down, so I let myself roll off, only a heartbeat before the huge metal wheels rolled past me.

I held on to the first stone I could find to stop me from being twirled away by the gale.

This train didn't stop like the other ones, and a moment or two later the station was calm again. I walked away from the track, relieved that I'd made it. When I was a safe distance away, I opened my arms and looked up at the sky and the rain. With my eyes closed and my mouth open, I welcomed every drop that hit me, until I was pleasantly drenched.

I'd been longing for a good soaking ever since I left Orzo's home.

When the heavy downpour started to knock me off balance, I trudged over the gravel to shelter under the platform edge.

I felt like new, hopeful – and hungry! But the ground I was standing on was littered with rusty debris, oil stains, sweet wrappers and rubbish of all kinds – not very appetising.

I had to choose a direction away from the station. To one side there was the familiar sight of the  tunnel: was it the same one I'd seen with Orzo and Tosca? I couldn't tell.

I started to walk down the platform, and by the time I got to the end, it was night. The storm hadn't stopped yet, and a rivulet had formed along the track, stopping me from going any further. From time to time the sky was lit up by lightning, and the huge claps of thunder that followed were quite scary. I had to find a safe place for the night, so I backed into a small crack in the concrete wall. I was uncomfortable, but safe, and as I lay there I

began to remember the wonderful times I used to have at home with Alma. One mistake had completely ruined my life. I found myself apologising to her, and I hoped that she could somehow hear my thoughts.

Then I realised that I wasn't alone. A little spider came crawling over my foot and perched on my knee. He reminded me of Big Mama Spider, back in my playhouse. I stroked him, and told him my story. Other creatures joined me – beetles, moths and roly-polies – and they all listened quietly to my sad tale.

As the storm faded into the distance, so did my hopes of finding my way home. Discouraged, and with a knot in my stomach, I fell asleep.

Chapter 23

Chased by Cubs

When I woke up, it was early morning, and the little gathering around me had dispersed. The clear, fresh air promised a beautiful sunny day, and the rain the night before had lifted my mood. But as soon as I stepped out of the crack, I saw that my feet and legs had become ridiculously hairy, with long white filaments growing from them. Not only did this creep me out, but I couldn't even walk properly. I pulled the hairs off and threw them away. More green sprouts were poking out of the skin on my arms and body. I decided to ignore what was happening to me and stay focused on my journey.

But I didn't know what to do. Wait for people to arrive again and try to get their attention? Or would I be wasting my time?

The walls to the top of the platform were impossible to climb. What should I do? You see, I was so hungry that my stomach was rumbling and I couldn't think clearly. I needed to eat something.

There was a good clump of grass and brambles by the railway tracks, over towards the tunnel. Surely there had to be some decent earth down there?

I walked towards it, my leaves bouncing with each step, until I was within reach of what was surely going to be a delicious soily snack.

On the way, I passed some discarded railway materials. And under a rusty metal sheet, I spotted the den

of a mother fox with her four little cubs. She seemed tired, but her cubs wouldn't let her rest.

Maybe she was the same fox that had attacked us, days ago? If she saw me, she'd surely tear me apart. I remembered how strong she was when we were tumbling helplessly around inside that old plastic bottle.

I stood still, terrified by being so close to them, and watching the cubs prancing and capering with each other. Finally their mother lay down and the cubs cuddled up around her. They looked adorable: their bond was the same as mine with Alma. For a moment I forgot about my fears and lost myself in the thought that we were all living beings, and so similar in many ways.

I was waiting for them to doze off when another train rolled past. It twirled me up in the air, and I landed close to the foxes. Just as I was getting up again, one of the cubs turned his head and saw me. I froze, and waited for him to go back to sleep. My heart was pounding. As soon as he put his head

down again, I sprinted towards the brambles.
But, from the corner of my eye, I saw the cub
getting up: he had seen me moving away. I heard
his bark, a horrible, screeching sound. I ran as fast
as I could, my legs hardly touching the ground,
but he was gaining on me. And the other cubs were
following him.

I reached the brambles and plunged into the undergrowth. The cub also dived in, but the thorns were too much for a little fox and he stopped chasing me. I moved further inside, until I felt I was safe. The four cubs lingered around the prickly bush, until their mother yelped at them. Her cries sounded like a baby in pain. The cubs ran back to her. My legs were shaky, my heart was throbbing – and my stomach was still rumbling! I fell to the ground. The dark soil was moist and soft. I scraped it up with my bare hands, and voraciously gobbled one mouthful after another. When I felt satisfied, I sat back and considered my next move. I had to get to the tunnel. From there, I could reach the street again and show myself to a human.

To be safe, I was going to trek along the line underneath the brambles.

It was a very long walk, and at the end of it I was met by a tall brick wall. The familiar litter that humans casually discard was all around me. I was next to the huge, dark entrance to the tunnel, but there was no way I could climb to the top of it.

I had hoped to be able to walk up the embankment

and find the place where we'd camped in the bottle on the other side. But the sun had already set, and the faint light coming from the other end of the tunnel would soon fade. I had to wait until the next day.

I looked for a shelter amongst the rubbish, and found a plastic dish, probably thrown there by children. It was full of water. As I lowered my head to drink from it, I saw myself reflected in the water: my leaves had grown a lot, and my hair seemed to have almost disappeared into them. My face looked thin and tired. I could hardly recognise myself.

After quenching my thirst, I turned the dish over and pulled it on top of a squashed beer can. Then I hid underneath it, hoping that I wouldn't get another visit from the foxes.

Chapter 24

The Tunnel

When the morning came, I had to pull the white roots off my legs again. Then I went to the entrance of the tunnel. A cool breeze was blowing out of it, like the breath from a gigantic mouth that was about to swallow me.

I clenched my fists and, with my gaze fixed on the light at the far end of the tunnel, I marched into it, determined to conquer this monster.

After I'd walked some way into the tunnel, I began to hear the fluttering of bats, and water trickling from the arched ceiling.

I remembered a song that Alma used to sing me, but I made up new words for it as I went along:

'Fly me from this gloom,
And let me get away from bats!
Let me see what life is like without marauding cats!
In other words, hold my leaves!
In other words, sunrays, kiss me!'

My little voice echoed loudly around the big, dark, empty space, filling it with my presence.
Soon it was so dark that I couldn't see the gravel of the railway track any more, and I had to feel my way using my hands.
Trains rolled by regularly, and I had to duck every time and hold on to a stone to stop the wind from blowing me away.

And I kept on singing, as loudly as I could.
Midway through my journey, when the light at
the end of the tunnel was the same size as the one
I'd left behind, I stopped, out of breath, thinking
about how far I had left to walk. It was scary to be
there, alone in the darkness.

Another train shot by, with its immense roar and
hurricane of air. This time I lost my grip, slammed
against the wall, and fell into a muddy puddle. I
was cold and shaken.

What if I were to die right there? Nobody would
know. Life would carry on as usual, with or
without me.

I realised that I was losing faith in myself, and I hated feeling that way. So I got up and stubbornly marched on, faster than before. But my mind was still racing with doubts. If I were to get out and find my way home, what then? I was probably destined to become a tree anyway. I could be a tree anywhere. Why was I trying so hard?

Trying to fend off these horrible thoughts, I sang louder and kept on over the wet stones. But it was hard to walk in the darkness: I was slipping and stumbling, until I fell badly, bruising myself.

I sobbed for a moment, lying there on my hands and knees.

Bats were now flying around the tunnel, and it sounded as if they were laughing. Was their laughter aimed at me?

I got to my feet again.

'How dare you?!' I shouted at them. 'Don't you have any feelings?!'

I dried my tears and forced myself onwards, surrounded by their creepy laughter. It was a struggle to keep going, but my annoyance at their bad manners gave me energy.

I wasn't going to let them mock me. I was still alive, and my future was waiting for me somewhere outside the tunnel.

Finally, I reached the exit, and the warm rays of the sun filled me with relief.

I could still hear the distant laughter of the bats behind me. Maybe they weren't having a go at me, after all. Either way, I had finally made it out. But when I scanned the steep banks of the railway line, I saw that I wasn't where I'd hoped to be at all. None of the trees or the buildings matched the places I'd seen with Orzo and Tosca. It seemed only the rubbish was the same. I looked up the steep slope, at the top of which stood a row of houses. Surely I would meet a human there?

I was exhausted, but I had to try. So I climbed the embankment, holding on to branches and stepping over litter, sticks and dead leaves.

I finally reached the road and stepped out on to the pavement. I had to catch my breath, but I was happy to have made it. I was on a very quiet village street. No one was nearby. But further down the road, I could see a church and a crossroads, and people moving around.

I ran towards them.

Chapter 25

The Broos

There were several humans ahead of me, some strolling, some striding along quickly, and some sprinting past on bikes.

As I ran towards them, I passed a small park. A shaggy old man was sitting on a bench, throwing pieces of bread to a dozen or so pigeons, which were pecking around his feet.

'Broo?' said a familiar voice.

I turned, and there she was.

'Broona? Is that you?' I asked.

'Broo!' the pigeon said, nodding its head. Broona waddled toward me.

'Broo… broo…' she repeated.

'Broona, we had a deal! But you never came back,' I said. 'You left me there with Chicobroo!'

'Broo…' she said again.

'And then he left, too!' I said, with growing anger.

'Broo… broo…' she went on.

I was a short distance from the old man, who stared at me wide-eyed. I wasn't going to waste my time with Broona any more. I raised my arms and asked him for help, but as I walked towards him, he lifted his feet and threw a handful of bread at me. Before I could convince him that I didn't mean any harm, Broona picked me up and flew away with me in her beak.

'Broona! Not again, let me go! Put me down! Put me down!' I repeated.

Then I stopped, because I was scared that she'd do just that, and drop me.

'Actually, don't. Don't put me down!' I quickly cried instead.

After a short flight, she landed on an old chimney stack, next to a rusty antenna. Chicobroo was perched on the antenna. As soon as he saw me, he hopped down to meet me.

'Chico?' I said. 'Why did you leave me behind?'

'Broo?' Broona asked him, too.

Chicobroo was noticeably nervous and somewhat embarrassed by his mother's stern look.

Broona pecked his tail.

'You told me she was broo!' she shouted at him.

'But I brooed she was broo!!' he argued back.

'Where did you broo her? Broo me!' she insisted.

The two squabbled for a bit, and finally Chico told us what had happened.

After the train incident he'd panicked and flown away, only to come back later in the day. He saw me lying on the track, senseless, but he couldn't fly down to me: he was too terrified of the trains. He watched me for a long time, and when I didn't move he assumed that I was dead. So he left, feeling sad and guilty. The next day, he flew over the station again and saw that I'd gone. He scouted the area near the station, and when he couldn't find me he thought the storm had blown me far away, into some dismal crack along the railway track or under a bush. And that's exactly where I was, under the brambles, where the foxes chased me.

When I'd heard his story, I couldn't hold a grudge against him.

I also questioned Broona, as she'd promised to fetch me too. She said she'd come back to the nest,

but had found it empty. She assumed that
Chicobroo had taken care of me, but when she
found him, he'd told her I was dead.

'Broona, we had a deal,' I told her. 'Your son can
fly, he's out of your nest now. And I really need to
get home.'

I wanted Broona to take me back to my home but
she wanted her son to make it up to me.

'Broo her back right now! And be broo to her,' she
ordered him.

Broona didn't have to insist. In fact, Chico was so
relieved to see me alive that he immediately
offered me his back. For a moment I hesitated.

'All right then, let's give it another go. But please
be careful this time, Chico. Stay focused,' I said, as
I sat between his wings. 'I know what my garden
looks like. As soon as I see it I'll tell you, OK?'

He took off, struggling to fly straight at first, but then he found his pace.

The air through my leaves and the beautiful sunlight filled me with joy. Could I really be close to getting home again?

As we circled the neighbourhood I described the trees in my garden, especially the big mimosa tree. I told him about my playhouse, the old shed, and the grey stone slabs in the middle of the garden. Admittedly, my house wasn't that unusual, and the trees looked quite similar to all the others from above.

'I can't broo any more… huff! I'm too broo…' he said, out of breath.

'No, wait!' I shouted. 'I think I just saw it! Over there! That's my playhouse! That's it! That's my home!'

He crash-landed in the mimosa tree, and I hugged him fondly.

'Please… let me broo…' he coughed.

'You're a star! Thank you!' I said, dismounting.

There it was: my playhouse. And my dear old garden. Nothing had changed; it just looked a bit

drier, and the grass was taller.

I couldn't wait to see Alma, hug her again, say how sorry I was for having been so silly, and tell her everything I'd been through.

Then I noticed that the windows didn't have curtains, and the rooms seemed empty.

We flew to the front of the house and checked again: it clearly looked as if it had been vacated. And the car was gone too.

Was it possible that Alma and her family didn't live here any more?

Chapter 26

Home Alone

My mind wrestled with what I was seeing. Where had they gone? It felt like a bad dream.

I asked Chicobroo to take me to the playhouse. I'd wait there in case Alma and her family came back. He left me on the branch next to the knothole which had been my doorway into the garden, a long time ago.

'Chico, we need to find out what happened. Please see if anyone round here knows anything.'

He left, promising that he'd visit me every day with any news. I went into the playhouse, my old home, through the knothole.

The place looked much tidier than I remembered. All my things were still there, and one of my pots had been left filled with water. Right next to it, there were the hazelnuts, the same ones I'd used to play with Spritz. A photo of me was pinned to the wooden wall, wearing a nice dress Alma had made for me. Below it, a little heart shaped note read: *Almondine lived here.*

I looked around for my old friends. They were hesitant at first, but as soon as they recognised me they all came out to greet me.

There was Emmelina with her funny, pointy wings, Herald, Tabby, Etiella, and furry Tabby and Gypsy.

Big Mama Spider and Daddy Long Legs joined us too. Gonzo, Zippy and Stinky were also still around and due to arrive later in the evening.

They all gathered around me, intrigued and

fascinated. Some felt me with their antennae, some touched me with their little paws, and some even crawled over my leaves.

I told them about the adventures I'd had, the places I'd seen and the people I'd met. Then I asked what had happened to Alma and her family. Had they seen her? Why was the house closed?

They looked at each other, as if afraid to break the news to me. Then Big Mama Spider spoke out, saying that nobody had come into the garden for quite some time. All the humans had gone not long after I had disappeared. Then the girl briefly came back one afternoon and that was it.

When night came, activity filled the garden, but I was content to stay in my home. I lay down on the old wooden spoon I used for a bed, but now I found it uncomfortable. I'd outgrown it, and my leaves were so long that they almost made me fall out of it. I preferred to stay up straight, so I simply sat near the window, and that's how I slept.

When I woke up, white filaments had grown out of my feet again. I pulled them off. As I got up, my back felt woodier than before, and my body ached when I tried to stretch it.

Then I heard loud tapping on the window.

It was Chicobroo, and it seemed that he had something urgent to tell me.

I went out through the knothole and stood on the branch next to him.

He'd found out from the blue tits that the family had returned from holiday, packed a big van with lots of boxes, and then left again.

'But when are they coming back?' I asked.

'They didn't broo that,' he said.

As we spoke, I saw that there were people inside the house. But my joy didn't last long. A man in a suit who I didn't recognise was showing a couple of other strangers around.

'This can't be possible. Have I really been away so long that the house is up for sale?' I said. 'Alma didn't tell me anything about leaving. What am I going to do now, Chicobroo?'

My mind was racing.

'I don't broo. Maybe broo a bit longer?' he said. He was probably right: what else could I do, anyway? I could only stay there and wait. But the thought of doing nothing disheartened me. You see, not only I was losing hope of ever seeing Alma again, I also feared how very soon I'd no longer be the Almondine she knew – I'd be a tree.

Chapter 27

The Hole

My dreams of seeing Alma again crumbled a little more with every hour that passed.

Meanwhile, my friends carried on with their lives. Big Mama Spider told me that the night brings good counsel, but it didn't. Not to me, anyway, not any more. All it brought was more long white roots growing from my feet. Three nights passed, and each morning I had to pull that weird hair off my legs.

On the fourth morning, I didn't bother.

I stayed indoors all the time, waiting for the door to swing open, imagining myself hugging Alma again. But she never came. Nothing happened around me, but my body didn't stop changing. Tosca's words kept coming back to me: that I shouldn't be afraid of my destiny.

I was still holding on to the past, except I was thinner, weaker, stiffer and loaded down with leaves. Who was I kidding? I wasn't Almondine any more.

I took one last look at what had once been my home, then squeezed out of the knothole, never to come back again.

I walked to a clear area at the end of the garden, some way from the other trees, and started to dig a hole with my hands.

Chicobroo arrived, as he did every morning, to tell me if there was any news.

'What are you brooing?' he said.

'It's time for me to become what I am,' I told him.

'Broo?'

'I'm a tree, Chico. And this is where a tree goes.'

'Broo? After all you've brooed to broo back here?'

'Look at me! Can't you see? There's no point fighting my destiny,' I said, showing him my body. 'Soon, I'll be a tree! Just like any other one.'

Chicobroo looked on, puzzled, while I stood in the hole and started covering my feet and legs with soil, right up to my knees.

'So, you're going to broo there?' he asked.

'That's it,' I said, lifting my arms as if they were two branches.

'That's broo, because I came to tell you they are broo! A broo girl has just arrived with her brooes. They are inside.'

Were these the new owners, or had Alma's family come back?

The door to the garden opened, and Alma walked out. Chicobroo took off and landed on the mimosa tree.

Alma went into the playhouse. My heart was throbbing. She came out, taking small cautious steps, and glanced around the garden, towards the shrubs and trees, and then to the ground.

I waved and tried to call her, but my voice choked.

Her eyes fell on me for a moment, and then she looked elsewhere. I tried to clear my throat and call her again, but her mum yelled from the house, telling her to get back inside.

Alma walked away, still looking around the garden, then closed the door behind her.

Chicobroo landed next to me, super-excited.

'What are you brooing in there, let's broo!'

'She didn't even see me,' I said.

The grim reality of what I'd become was dawning on me.

'It doesn't broo! You want to see her, broo?'

'I'm a twig, a stick, just another plant! It's too late, Chico. Forget it.'

Chicobroo cocked his head as if I'd somehow given him an idea.

'Don't listen to your brooes…' he said. 'You need to broo in yourself, I really do broo in you and…'

'Chico, it would just freak her out!' I interrupted. 'And make her sad. It's better that she remembers me as I was. It can't be the same, now: me and Alma, together, having fun, like two friends. That's all gone.'

I realised that I was crying.

'But you want to see her, broo?' Chico asked again, still confused.

I saw Alma lifting the sash window in her bedroom. She looked down the garden for a moment, then moved inside.

'Broo? You want to see her! Broo?' he repeated.

'Yes, Chico,' I said, against my will, weeping.

'Then, let's broo! And stop brooing!' he said.

He helped me get out of the hole I'd dug. As I cleaned the soil off my legs, I also pulled off the white roots tangled around them.

I mounted his back and dried my eyes.

'Let's go,' I said.

Chapter 28

Reunion

We landed on the window sill of her bedroom.
'Wait,' I told him.

Alma was sitting on the floor of her empty room,
looking through our old photos. Was I doing the
right thing? I wasn't the girl in the pictures any
more. But my need to hug her again, and tell her
how much I loved her, conquered any doubts I
had left.

I knocked on the glass.

I can still remember how she jumped when she
saw us. She was scared for a moment, but then she
rushed over to lift the sash window. I dismounted
from Chicobroo, and he flew off. And now it was

just the two of us again as before.

'Almondine? Is it really you?' she said. For a moment my heart sank. She was frowning, and I thought she was unhappy to see what I'd become. But she wasn't angry, she was just worried.

She took me in the palm of her hand,

and her face beamed with her biggest-ever smile. She told me how happy she was to see me, and asked if I was feeling well.

I told her the truth: I was well, but I no longer felt like the girl I used to be.

She stroked my leaves. To my surprise, she seemed to like them.

She wanted to know what had happened to me since the day I'd disappeared, and so I began to tell her my story.

Then her mum called her again.

'Alma! Come on, or we'll miss the plane!'

Alma wanted to put me in a box, so she could take me with her.

'No, stop, please!' I said. 'I'm going to stay here.'

'What do you mean?' she said. 'Why?'

'I'm going to turn into a tree, and I don't want you to see that. Leave me here. I'm just happy that I was able to see you again.'

'But, Almondine, I can't just leave you here!' she said her face becoming sad. 'Please come with me. We're going far away, to America.'

'It won't be like it used to be,' I said. 'I'm a sapling.'

'But that's OK!' Alma exclaimed. 'I can look after you. I'd love to do that.'

'But I'll be a tree,' I said.

'Even if you are a tree!'

But I insisted that I couldn't go. Alma wiped tears from her eyes. I think she remembered how upset

I'd become when she locked me in the drawer. She didn't want to argue with me again. As hard as it was, she was going to respect my decision.

I hugged her fondly, just like I used to.

She put me on the window ledge, and almost immediately Chicobroo landed next to me. I climbed on to his back, and we flew off.

Alma was smiling. And crying at the same time. And so was I.

Chapter 29

Almondine's Destiny

We landed in exactly the spot where I'd been planting myself.

I dismounted and silently began to clear the hole.

'I don't broo it… Broo! What are you brooing?' Chicobroo asked.

'Starting my new life,' I said, continuing to dig. 'This is where I belong… this is my destiny. I'm not afraid.'

I kept repeating Tosca's last words to myself: 'Whatever it takes… you don't have to be afraid of your destiny…'

'Broostiny?'

'Yes, Chico, destiny. It's like saying your future.

Everyone has a future.'

'Broo-ture?'

'A future that is our own… no one else's. And this is mine.'

'Broo?'

'This is what I'm meant to be. It's why I exist. I came from a tree. I'll stay here, and live the rest of my life as one,' I said with a heavy heart.

'So you broo yourself in the broo,' he said.

'That's it,' I said.

'What a broo! After all your friends have brooed for you,' he said sadly. 'All the ones who loved you.'

That word suddenly hit me: love.

I remembered Tosca saying how my love had changed her destiny.

It had seemed normal for me to help her at the time, but now I wasn't helping anybody: I was ignoring what my heart really wanted. And what Alma wanted.

What was I doing? Was this really love? Had I forgotten what I meant to her? This wasn't just about me!

I stared at my feet in the hole where I'd stand, all alone, from now on. And I thought: where was love in all this?

'Chico, you're right.' I said. 'Life has to have

meaning, but not just to ourselves. Also to the people we love!'

'Broo?'

'Alma didn't care how much I'd changed, or what I'm going to become. Because she loves me.'

'She broos,' he said cocking his head.

'And I love her, too,' I said.

'Broo… So, what do you want to broo?'

'Broo me back to her!' I said.

Chapter 30

Back to Alma!

We went back to her window, but the room was empty. Then we looked at the front of the house: they'd already left!

We flew over the nearby streets, but it was impossible to tell where they'd gone.

We turned back and landed on a shrub in the front garden. I was so frustrated.

Spritz was walking down the pavement, and he saw us.

'Not him again,' I said.

He stalked under the shrub and sat looking straight up at us.

Was my life circling right back to where all my

troubles began? It seemed like nothing had changed for the better. But that was when my luck turned.

A white taxi pulled up in front of the house. There was a stranger in the driver's seat, but Alma's dad was sitting next 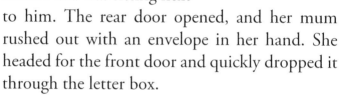 to him. The rear door opened, and her mum rushed out with an envelope in her hand. She headed for the front door and quickly dropped it through the letter box.

I could see Alma on the back seat, staring down at something on her lap.

'It's them! Stop them, Chico! Don't let them go!' I shouted, getting on his back.

Chico landed on the bonnet of the car and started hopping around and flapping his wings, shocking Alma's mum, who screamed as she started to get into the car.

The driver turned on the windscreen wipers to scare us away and Chico slipped on the bonnet, making me fall to the ground next to one of the wheels. It was a big drop, but my long leaves

softened the impact. Chico went on hopping around on the bonnet, flapping his wings to distract their attention.

From where I stood, I could see Spritz slinking towards me.

The driver opened the door and went to hush Chicobroo away.

Alma knew what was going on. She got out of the car and rushed to the front wheel, where I'd fallen. She picked me up and quickly hid me in the big pocket of her jacket.

Suddenly, I was in pitch darkness.

I heard Alma's father telling her to get back in the car, wings fluttering, and Spritz meowing.

He sounded annoyed. Then the doors all slammed, the seat belts clicked, and the car drove off. They were all wondering what they'd just seen. Alma's mum was worried that it might be something to do with the car.

The driver chuckled: he said the bird must have eaten something that disagreed with it. Alma's dad asked her what she'd picked up from the ground. She pretended that she'd been looking for a stone to throw at the bird, but couldn't find one. I giggled.

Snug inside the pocket, I could feel the weight of her hand resting on top of me, just like it had when I was born.

I wanted to thank Chico for all he'd done. I'd never have thought that he could be so brave. But I was leaving him behind, and I'd probably never see him again. And it was the same with everyone else: my friends in the playhouse, cheeky little Orzo and his family, wise old Tosca, earnest

Sergeant Spencer, and Spritz. Well, I was quite relieved to leave him behind.

I felt safe, though, and excited again.

Amongst the chatter in the car, I heard Alma's voice saying: 'We'll be fine.'

I knew she wasn't talking to her parents. She was talking to me. *We* were going to be fine.

Her fingers reached down into the pocket, searching for me.

I hugged them, and I was happy.

Epilogue

After a very long journey, they all arrived at their new home.

Almondine had no idea where they were, but she loved the weather and the bright, hot sun. Best of all was their new garden, so big and lush.

By the time Alma finished writing down this story in a diary, Almondine was no longer able to walk but she could still speak, with her little mouth appearing out of the bark.

Alma was intrigued by how well Almondine overcame her problems, because she was soon going to be a teenager herself and Almondine's journey gave her courage – as well as enthusiasm and curiosity.

She thought she'd better be careful who she played with: even in her world there might be a Spritz who'd want to toy with her.

But the one thing she heard from her tiny friend that impressed her the most was that, even in her miniature world, there was so much love to give. Sometimes it was hidden behind strange habits and difficult to see, but it was there.

And Almondine was always able to find it.

And eventually she found it for herself, too.

She'd accepted herself for who she really was: not a weird, ugly quirk of nature, but someone who was able to love.

And that's because, in the end, love is the one thing that makes us truly happy.

Almondine's Transformation

Here is the complete progression of how Almondine has changed up until now.

We can call this transformation a *metamorphosis*, an old Greek word made from *"meta"* (change) and *"morphē"* (shape).

A Roman poet called Ovid wrote a massive book by the same name in which he tells of more than two hundred myths involving a metamorphosis. Yes, the ancients had a wild imagination when it came to fantastical transformations!

But this happens a lot in nature too! In fact, some of the most common animals dramatically change their form at one or more stages during their development.

Can you name ten creatures that undergo a metamorphosis before reaching their adulthood?

Think of insects, fish, amphibians, molluscs or crustaceans.

See the page on the right for some clues!

Please write a review

Please let Gabriele Zucchelli know what you thought about
Almondine by leaving your review on the online store where
you bought this book.

If you are under age 13 please ask a grown up to help you.

Discover more!

For more information, bonus material, activities and other
curiosities, please visit **almondine.club**

Social Media

The Author is aware of some of the concerns surrounding
the potentially addictive use of social media and is not an
advocate of such platforms in general for children.
If you are the parent and if you are happy to contribute to
the books' visibility with a Comment or 'Like',
you can find the links on:
almondine.club

Thank you!

About the Author

Gabriele grew up in Italy where he discovered the awesome art of animation when he was only twelve years old.
Some years later in Milan, he met some very talented animators, who became his first teachers. He hasn't stopped animating and working in this field ever since.

He's worked on a lot of well-known films ever since moving to London, firstly using pencil and paper, and later with computers. More than twenty-five years have now passed since his first job in the UK – the animated version of *Peter Rabbit and Friends* – and the more recent ones – *The Jungle Book* and *The Lion King*.
A few years ago he also directed a historical documentary on the first ever animated feature films: *Quirino Cristiani*.

The *Almondine* trilogy is his first work as an author of children's books.

Find out the rest of Almondine's story in the other two books:

ALMONDINE
Book 1

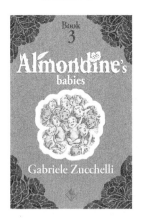

ALMONDINE'S BABIES
Book 3

My Thoughts and Drawings

Would you like to share your thoughts and pictures?
Take a snapshot and ask a grown-up to share it on the blog at:
almondine.club

Cut your Bookmark!

Book 2

Printed in Great Britain
by Amazon